His body was warm and male against hers.

Just when she thought for sure he was going to kiss her, he released her and stepped back. “I’ll be free by two o’clock tomorrow. We could go for a drive.”

“What if I drop by the guest house?” she said. A drive wouldn’t work for what she had in mind.

“Are you propositioning me, Brie? How naughty.”

Her cheeks flamed, not that he could tell in the dark. “Don’t be silly. You’re not so irresistible that I have to jump your bones hours after you come back to town.”

“I’m devastated.” He put a hand to his chest jokingly, as if she had dealt him a mortal wound. “The Brie I remember was not so cruel.”

“I have to go,” she said. “Will you be there when I show up?”

“I’ll be waiting, Brie. Can’t wait to see what happens.”

* * *

Too Texan to Tame by Janice Maynard is part of the Texas Cattleman’s Club: Inheritance series.

Dear Reader,

Being a parent is never easy. I've often wondered how single moms and dads do it. I suspect it's with a circle of support and a host of sleepless nights.

My heroine, Brielle, is trying very hard to do the right thing for her daughter. She thinks the little girl needs *two* parents, but Brie is not at all sure that Vaughn Blackwood is daddy material.

I hope you enjoy this tale of two star-crossed lovers who messed things up the first time around. Parenthood can make or break their new relationship, and the stakes are high.

Things are always hotter in Texas! :)

Happy reading!

Janice Maynard

JANICE MAYNARD

TOO TEXAN TO TAME

Special thanks and acknowledgment are given to Janice Maynard for her contribution to the Texas Cattleman's Club: Inheritance miniseries.

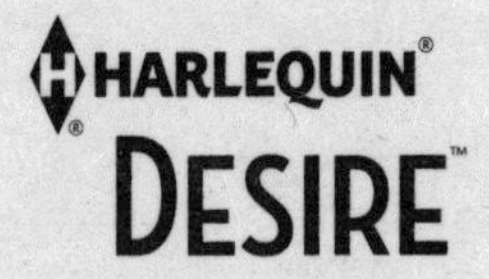

ISBN-13: 978-1-335-20902-3

Too Texan to Tame

This edition published by arrangement with Harlequin Books S.A.

For questions and comments about the quality of this book, please contact us at CustomerService@Harlequin.com.

Harlequin Enterprises ULC
22 Adelaide St. West, 40th Floor
Toronto, Ontario M5H 4E3, Canada
www.Harlequin.com

Printed in U.S.A.

USA TODAY bestselling author **Janice Maynard** loved books and writing even as a child. After multiple rejections, she finally sold her first manuscript! Since then, she has written fifty-plus books and novellas. Janice lives in Tennessee with her husband, Charles. They love hiking, traveling and family time.

You can connect with Janice at www.janicemaynard.com, www.Twitter.com/janicemaynard, www.Facebook.com/janicemaynardreaderpage, www.Facebook.com/janicesmaynard and www.Instagram.com/therealjanicemaynard.

Books by Janice Maynard

Harlequin Desire

Southern Secrets

Blame It On Christmas
A Contract Seduction
Bombshell for the Black Sheep

Texas Cattleman's Club: Inheritance

Too Texan to Tame

Visit her Author Profile page at Harlequin.com, or janicemaynard.com, for more titles.

You can also find Janice Maynard on Facebook, along with other Harlequin Desire authors, at Facebook.com/harlequindesireauthors!

For Caroline and Anna.
You two are the best mothers I know. :)

Love always,

Mom

One

Vaughn Blackwood would do just about anything for his baby sister, Sophie, even if it meant returning to Royal, Texas. Again. He'd been back far too often lately. A New Year's Eve ball—because Sophie had begged. Before that, for his father's funeral. And, of course, the reading of the will. Hell, that had been a disaster.

His father's legal adviser, Kace LeBlanc, was Vaughn's age, give or take. But if LeBlanc had any sympathy toward the heirs who had come up empty-handed, he hadn't shown it. After all, the guy was a lawyer. He probably wouldn't bleed if you cut him.

LeBlanc wasn't a bad guy, but he sure as hell was a pro at handing out bad news. Buckley Blackwood hadn't left his dear children so much as two pennies to rub together. His entire estate had gone to Miranda Blackwood, the second of Buckley's ex-wives.

The whole situation was a travesty of justice. Just because Vaughn didn't want anything from his father didn't mean it was okay for his siblings Kellan and Sophie to get the shaft.

He gripped the steering wheel, absently noting the familiar landmarks as he got closer to town. In between his bouts of indignation, other feelings simmered uncomfortably. Vaughn hadn't adored his father. No warm, fuzzy childhood memories lingered. But he'd never wanted the man dead. In fact, when he first heard the news that Buckley "Buck" Blackwood had passed, Vaughn actually felt something twist in his chest. A sharp pang of regret. The bittersweet knowledge that some fences would never be mended now.

Then he'd attended the will reading and had been sharply reminded of why he and the old man were never close. His father had been a hard-nosed son of a bitch. So it wasn't entirely surprising that even from the grave, Buck was manipulating and shortchanging his own flesh and blood.

Vaughn had done his damnedest to avoid all the inheritance drama back home. As far as he was concerned, Miranda, the stepwitch, as they called her, could spend the old man's riches however she wanted. It was a sweet pot of gold, for sure. First, there was Blackwood Bank—the family business. Then a series of homes all over the globe. The seven-figure fortune. And last but not least, Blackwood Hollow, the sprawling ranch outside Royal.

If Vaughn had any regrets at all about being shut out of his father's will, it was only the thought of never visiting the ranch again. He'd met Brielle there. Some days those memories were sweet. Other days they made him angry. And occasionally, like today, they made him ache.

Stubbornly, he pushed all thoughts of Brie aside. She was a mistake. Relegated to his past. For his peace of mind, she needed to stay there. Vaughn had left Royal, Texas—and Brielle—a long time ago, and he had set out to make his own mark in the world, away from his father's long shadow. He'd earned his first million buying up land in the Fort Worth area and selling drilling rights. His company, Blackwood Energy Corp., was worth $500 million by most recent estimates. Royal, Texas, might be where his life began, but Vaughn had moved on.

He parked his late-model Mercedes—the one he kept in a fancy garage at the airport for his visits—in front of the elegant country guesthouse that would be his base for the next week or so. His hostess, Dixie Musgraves, owned this building and all of Magnolia Acres. As a longtime friend of the Blackwood family, she had supported Kellan, Sophie and Vaughn since they were kids. She had also stepped in as a second mother when their own mother died of a stroke a few years ago.

Now, the attractive fiftysomething redhead came out to meet him. She hugged him tightly. "I've missed you, sweet boy."

"Hey, Dixie." Vaughn grinned, returning the warm embrace. This "boy" towered over her by almost a foot.

Dixie had been a dear friend to Donna-Leigh Blackwood since before Vaughn and his siblings were born and had loved and cared for Donna-Leigh all the way to the day she died. Actually, the name had been Donna-Leigh Westbrook by then. Vaughn's mother had taken back her maiden name as a postdivorce jab at her controlling ex-husband. The public action had made Buck seethe, but Donna-Leigh had been beyond his touch by then.

Buck Blackwood was a distant parent on his best days, a harsh, punishing father on his worst. Since Donna-Leigh's passing, Dixie had been the closest thing the Blackwood kids had to a nurturing figure in their lives.

She grabbed his smallest bag. "Come on in, honey. I've got iced tea and beer and anything else you want."

Vaughn reached for his high-end leather backpack and large suitcase, following her into the house. It had been months since he felt so relaxed. Despite the many family situations brewing, it was good to be home…to be back in Royal.

He set the luggage at the foot of the stairs. "I'm still thankful the wildfires spared Magnolia Acres," he said. "Is everything here going well?" He sprawled in an easy chair and accepted the glass she handed him. "Thanks, Dixie."

"Yep," she said. "We're right as rain, pardon the pun. Word has rippled through town about the two fire crews you funded and sent. And that you came yourself. People are grateful."

Guilt curled in his stomach. "Well, it seemed the least I could do," he muttered, grimacing.

Dixie cocked her head and gave him the stink eye. "And now here you are. You didn't want to come again so soon, did you?"

He shrugged. "Not particularly. But when a man's sister gets married, he doesn't have much choice."

Her gaze softened. "Sophie will be so glad you're here. Your brother will, too. And Darius is coming with Audra."

"We keep missing each other."

Her sympathetic gaze told him she saw his inward turmoil. "He's a great guy. You'll like him when the two of you have the chance to bond."

"I'm sure I will." His words were deliberately bland. These last few months had been filled with too much drama. Too many surprises. Like discovering he had a half brother. He hadn't fully adjusted to the status quo. So he decided to change the subject.

But Dixie wasn't going to let him act like his normal taciturn self. "Is that all you have to say?" she asked.

"I feel bad about Dad's will," he muttered, shrugging. "I never wanted anything of his for myself, but why give it all to Miranda? She must have done something to manipulate Dad."

"Give me your glass," she said. "You need some more tea. And maybe a scone. Low blood sugar is the only excuse I can think of for such crazy talk."

"She's Kellan's age, for God's sake. How can you stand up for her? She's nothing more than a gold digger."

Dixie handed him another drink and cuffed the side of his head. "Listen to me, you hardheaded Blackwood. Lord knows I loved your mother. She was like the sister I never had. But when Miranda hooked up with your father, the first marriage was legally over. Barely. You know it was."

"Doesn't mean Miranda is a saint."

"She signed a prenup. Walked away after the divorce without a penny of Blackwood money. And she's made a name for herself in the big city."

"What's your point?"

"Even though she had a heads-up before the will reading, I think Miranda was as shocked as any of you that Buck made her his sole heir."

He swirled the tea in his glass. "Maybe. It still seems fishy."

"So you're going to join Kellan and Sophie in contesting it?"

He looked up, shocked. "Me? No. I've got everything I need."

Dixie gave him a mysterious smile. "Maybe you do, and maybe you don't." She glanced at her watch. "Oh, shoot. I've gotta run. Make yourself at home, Vaughn. There's no one in the other bedroom. I know how you love your privacy."

He frowned. "What does that mean?"

"Not a thing, sweetie. Don't be so touchy."

He followed her to the porch. "Thanks for the hospitality, Dixie. I really appreciate it. With my brother a newlywed and my sister in the midst of wedding fever, it's nice to have a place to myself."

His hostess nodded. “Glad I can help.” She paused on the bottom step, shielding her eyes from the sun and staring up at him. “Did you know Brie is back in town?”

The news kicked him in the chest like a horse. Vaughn kept his expression neutral, but it wasn’t easy. “Oh?”

Dixie grinned smugly. “About six weeks ago now. She’s opened up a private practice veterinarian clinic on Main Street. Mostly for pets. Calls it Happy Trails. Seems to be doing well.”

“I thought she liked large animals and ranching.”

“I wouldn’t know about that. Your daddy sure was fond of her when she worked at Blackwood Hollow.”

So was I, Vaughn thought bleakly. But Brie had wanted and needed things he couldn’t give her.

Again, he kept his face and his tone carefully non-committal. “She definitely had a way with horses. You won’t find many ranch hands as gifted or as overqualified.”

“True. I suppose she was wasting her talent working for Buckley. He never did recognize her education or her value…at least not when it came to giving her a fair paycheck.”

“Tightfisted until the end.” Vaughn rubbed the back of his neck. Talking about his father and Brielle wasn’t helping the knot in his stomach. “I think I’ll grab a shower and go see Sophie.”

“You’re welcome to join me for dinner. I always have plenty.”

“Not tonight, but I appreciate it. I’ll take you up on

that invitation another evening. Thanks for rolling out the welcome mat."

Her grin was a tad wistful. "Maybe I'm hoping I can convince you to come home for good."

Vaughn shook his head slowly. "Not in the cards, Dixie."

She waved as she walked toward the main house, tossing a last shot over her shoulder. "Never say never."

Vaughn stood in a corner of his sister's enormous living room and eyed the crowd that ebbed and flowed around him. He'd been hoping for a private word with his sister. Apparently, private moments were in short supply during the days and weeks leading up to a wedding.

He was glad, at least, to see that Sophie looked amazing...and happy. The buttoned-up English fellow on her arm was her fiancé, Nigel Townshend.

Fortunately, the man seemed completely smitten with Vaughn's baby sister. It was a good thing, because if Vaughn had sensed any duplicity in the guy, he'd have been forced to beat the Brit to a pulp.

Sophie was innocent and sweet. Far too trusting. Not only that, but Buckley Blackwood had done a number on his only daughter's self-esteem, because he didn't know how to parent a girl.

Fortunately, Sophie had matured into a caring, lovely woman in spite of their father, and she deserved every bit of happiness she seemed to have found. Even so, the thought of this wedding to come made Vaughn jumpy. So much damn money and time and effort for a ceremony and a noose that experts predicted had a fifty-fifty shot at success.

Vaughn wasn't a pessimist. He was a realist.

Monogamy was not a natural state for the human species. His own father had sucked at marriage. Vaughn was briefly tempted once, but the woman had wised up and ditched him after he repeatedly insisted that wedded bliss wasn't his thing.

Remembering the expression on Brielle's face when she said her goodbyes eviscerated Vaughn to this day. But he couldn't regret his honesty with her. He'd only told her the unvarnished truth.

Moments later when Kellan appeared with his gorgeous Russian bride, Irina, at his side, Vaughn slammed the door on his negative thoughts and hugged his older brother. He kissed Irina on both cheeks. "Congrats on the baby-to-be."

Irina beamed. "We are so happy," she exclaimed. "Your brother is a wonderful man."

Kellan puffed out his chest. "Keep talking, sweet wife. I want Vaughn to hear all about how wonderful I am."

Vaughn snorted. "Somebody's been brainwashing her."

In the laughter that followed, Kellan kissed his wife's cheek, making her blush. Then he turned his attention back to Vaughn. "Did you know that Brielle is back in Royal?"

Seriously? This again? Why was everyone so obsessed with keeping Vaughn up-to-date about his ex-lover? He shrugged. "Dixie mentioned it."

Kellan lifted an eyebrow. “And?”

“And nothing. Brie and I were never serious.” The lie caught in his throat.

Kellan shook his head. “I’m not buying that. You were mad about her.”

Irina pinched her husband’s arm. “Why are you being so mean to your brother? Leave him alone.”

Vaughn was both touched and amused. “Thanks for the backup, Irina, but I can handle Kellan. We’ve been sparring partners since I was five—Kellan might have been three years older, but even then, I could hold my own. I’ve been able to bust his ass since I turned twelve.”

“Not true,” Kellan insisted, bristling theatrically.

Irina shook her head, rolling her eyes at both of them. “We will leave you on that note, dear Vaughn. It’s good that you are home where you belong.”

“I’m not *home*,” Vaughn insisted. But it was too late. They didn’t hear him. While the other couple walked away to do more socializing, Vaughn sighed and maintained his position.

As good as it was to see his family, this kind of crap was what he didn’t need. Come back to Royal for good? Not a chance.

Sophie breezed across the room in Vaughn’s direction. Earlier in the evening, Vaughn had met the British fiancé briefly. But now Sophie was on her own.

“Great party, sis,” he said. “Any chance you and I could have some time alone later?”

She waved a hand. “Maybe tomorrow. Noonish. We *do* need to catch up.” Despite her glowing mood, there were dark shadows beneath her eyes.

He curled an arm around her waist. "You look exhausted, Soph. Everything okay?"

She leaned her head on his shoulder and yawned. "Everything is perfect now that you're home. Did you know Brie is back in town?"

His jaw clenched. "Yeah. I heard."

"She's opened a vet clinic. I took Mr. Boots there for his shots last week. The whole waiting room was full."

The niggling headache Vaughn had earlier was turning into a full-blown drum line chorus. Before he could think of yet another innocuous response, a young, uniformed maid appeared. "Ms. Blackwood? There's someone at the front door asking to see Mr. Blackwood." The employee glanced at Vaughn. "Mr. *Vaughn* Blackwood."

Sophie yawned again. "Tell them to come in."

The maid fidgeted. "They don't want to intrude."

Vaughn interrupted. "I'll deal with it, sis." There was no way the mystery caller at the front door was Brielle. Why would she show up uninvited at Sophie's house? And looking for him, no less?

Despite the uneasiness in the pit of his stomach, he strode through the crowded rooms, not making eye contact with anyone. Maybe this was his chance to escape and go back to the blessedly quiet guesthouse.

When he put his hand on the doorknob and pulled, his spine tingled. As if lightning was about to strike the cold metal in his fingers. Nonsense. Absolute nonsense. "Can I help you?" he asked gruffly as he swung open the door.

Two

Brielle sucked in a shocked breath. She had asked to speak to Vaughn, but she hadn't held out much hope that he would come. "It's me," she said. And then realized that her words were foolish and bumbling. *Of course* Vaughn knew who she was.

He still held the edge of the door with one hand, the fingers white-knuckled. "Brielle."

Just the one word. Hoarse. Disbelieving.

Her lips twisted. "You seem shocked. I thought surely someone would have told you I've moved back to Royal."

"Oh, they have," he muttered. "A whole parade of 'em."

There was an odd note in his voice. And though it was hard to tell in the harsh glow of the porch light, he seemed pale.

He was as beautiful as she remembered. Thick brown hair, intense green eyes. And a clean-shaven jaw that would make a sculptor weep with envy. Her insides turned all shivery.

She shifted from one foot to the other. "I stopped by Magnolia Acres and asked Dixie where you were. One of my friends said she heard you blew into town last night."

"No secrets in Royal." Now he sounded almost bitter.

"I was sorry to hear about your dad. And his crazy will."

"No great loss. Clearly, we kids didn't mean that much to him."

"Surely he had his reasons."

"Did you come tonight to discuss my father?" The question was curt.

"You don't have to be rude."

He lifted his chin, closed his eyes briefly, then pinned her with a stare that practically froze her on the spot. "Why are you here, Brielle?"

She gnawed her lip. "I need to talk to you."

He waved a hand in a "go on" gesture. "Knock yourself out."

"Not now," she said. "Not in public."

His gaze narrowed. "I think you said everything I needed to hear the last time we were together. I'm a selfish Peter Pan with no compassion, no heart and no real purpose on the planet."

Brie winced. Hearing her own words quoted back to her made her feel slightly ill. "I was angry," she said.

"No kidding." Vaughn's steely-eyed gaze flayed her.

"I really do need to talk to you. It's important," she whispered, suddenly close to tears. She had never seen a man less open to mending fences. Animosity rolled off him in waves.

Vaughn glanced at his watch impatiently. "I need to get back to the party. The bride-to-be will be wondering where I am. Surely whatever this is can wait."

"I have a half day at the clinic tomorrow. Could we do lunch?"

He shook his head. "I already have a date with Sophie. And honestly, I'm not going to have much free time while I'm in Royal."

Wow. She hadn't expected this. It almost appeared as if her defection had actually hurt him. But why? He'd been the one dead set on making sure she knew the rules when it came to their relationship. Strictly temporary. Recreational sex. No promises. No future.

It wasn't as if he had been in love with her. "Never mind," she said dully.

As she turned to leave, he grabbed her arm. Not hard. But firmly. As if he really didn't want her to go. "Wait," he said. "I'm sorry. You caught me off guard." He closed the door behind him and led her down a couple of steps to the driveway below. "Is it really so important? I thought you hated my guts."

"I never hated you, Vaughn. We were simply too different to make things work."

Almost against his will—or so it seemed—he cupped her cheek in one large, warm palm. "You look beautiful, Brie." Something hovered between them for five seconds. Ten. Her legs trembled. Her breath lodged in her throat.

"I'm a mess," she protested. It was true. She had come straight from the clinic. It was her late night. She had put on a clean top, because her lab coat had been spattered with blood. Her hair was caught up in a loose knot. She hadn't had time to fix it.

His body was warm and male close to hers.

Just when she thought for sure he was going to kiss her, he stepped back. "I'll be free by two o'clock tomorrow. We could go for a drive."

The sudden concession dissipated some of the heavy, leaden feeling in her stomach. "What if I drop by the guesthouse?" she said. A drive wouldn't work for what she had in mind.

He raised an eyebrow. "Are you propositioning me, Brie?" His sardonic jab was meant to make her uncomfortable.

Her cheeks flamed—not that he could tell in the dark. "Don't be silly. You're not so irresistible that I have to jump your bones hours after you come back to town."

"I'm devastated," he said, clearly not serious. "The Brie I remember was not so cruel."

"I have to go," she said. "Will you be there when I show up?"

The sharp note in her voice didn't affect him at all. He had the gall to lift an eyebrow and give her a tight smile. "I'll be waiting, Brie. Can't wait to see what happens."

* * *

Vaughn stood on the porch and watched Brie's little car disappear down the driveway. He believed he'd put on a good show of being totally relaxed, but inside, he was less so.

What did she want from him? And why all the secrecy?

It occurred to him that she might need an investor for her veterinary practice. It wasn't easy these days to get a new business off the ground. But if that was the case, why ask *him*?

The questions swirled unanswered in his head as he went back inside and mingled. He had about reached his limits for socializing.

Nigel, Sophie's fiancé, and Irina, Kellan's pregnant bride, were holding court on the far side of the living room in a circle of admirers. The aristocratic television executive and the Russian former model were both magnetic personalities.

Meanwhile, Kellan and Sophie stood huddled in a nearby alcove, whispering. Vaughn joined them. "I think I'll head out," he said.

Sophie's face fell. "So soon?"

"I was up early," Vaughn said. "For a work meeting. I barely made it to the airport on time."

Kellan leaned against the wall, clearly keeping tabs on his wife across the expanse of expensive carpet. "I wish you had returned sooner and been able to meet Darius. He had an important meeting he couldn't miss in LA, so he and his girlfriend, Audra, headed to California a few days ago. They'll be back for the wedding, of course, but it would have been great if you could have spent time with him before then."

Vaughn experienced a jolt of relief. Things were complicated enough at the moment. He wasn't sorry to delay that odd family reunion with a stranger who shared his blood.

"What do we think of our half brother?" Vaughn asked.

Sophie and Kellan exchanged glances.

Kellan shrugged. "I like him. He's a straight-up guy. The DNA test results were conclusive."

Sophie nodded. "Darius is honestly as rattled as the rest of us. Can you imagine what it was like to hear that his biological father was Buck Blackwood?"

Kellan snorted. "And that despite the dramatic reveal, the old man left him nothing?"

"Where does Miranda fit into all this?" Vaughn asked. "I have a hard time imagining that she wants to deal with the ranch or the bank when her whole life is back in New York. She's got the TV show, for one thing. Plus, New York is the home base for her exercise empire. And since everyone knows she got the inheritance while we were left out in the cold, Royal can't possibly be a fun gig for her right now. Surely she doesn't need the money."

"Well, you do know that *Secret Lives* has been doing some filming here. Audiences love the whole Western angle," Sophie said.

Vaughn shook his head, filled with admiration and love for his sister. "I still can't believe you infiltrated the show and posed as a consultant."

Kellan grinned. "And got a husband out of it besides when you fell in love with the production company's CEO."

Sophie's smug smile told Vaughn that she didn't regret a thing. "I went there trying to dig up dirt on Miranda, but honestly, I think she's not as bad as we've painted her all this time."

Vaughn scowled. "And yet somehow she managed to inherit *everything* from a man who wasn't even her husband anymore. I'm not buying the innocent surprised act."

"I get where you're coming from," Kellan said. "But Miranda has dropped a few hints that the inheritance drama might not be over yet."

Sophie nodded. "When I was over at the house making last-minute wedding arrangements, she mentioned the word *caretaker*. As if something in the future will be different."

"Well, thank God it has nothing to do with me. As soon as you and Nigel are legally wed, I'm getting back to Fort Worth. I'm not waiting around to see if my dearly departed dad has some Machiavellian plan for my future."

Kellan sighed. "He died virtually alone. Didn't even let anyone know he was near the end. And because he had alienated his friends and family, he was left with nothing that mattered. Makes you feel kind of bad for him, doesn't it?"

Vaughn shook his head slowly. "You two are more forgiving than I am. He brought his troubles on himself."

"Maybe so," Sophie said. "But Kellan and I are so happy now, it's hard to hold a grudge."

Vaughn put an arm around each of them, closing the circle. "He may have been a wretched excuse for a father, but he and Mom gave us each other. I love you both. Now get back to the party and let me be an old curmudgeon in peace."

A half hour later, Vaughn pulled up in front of the guesthouse, got out of the car and stretched. The sky cradled a million stars tonight. Quite a change from the view he was used to. The Dallas/Fort Worth metroplex was his home these days. He loved the energy and vitality of the cities.

Even so, Royal's slower pace and laid-back charm drew him in, restored his sense of balance.

He couldn't help thinking of Brielle at this moment. How many times had the two of them indulged their love of amateur astronomy? How many times had they spread a quilt in some private field and made love under the stars?

The memories swamped him, coming as thick and fast as a flash flood in a dry gulch. She had been everything to him at one time. But he had been too driven, too ambitious. He'd let the relationship wither on the vine, leaving Brie to point out his shortcomings and ultimately to leave him.

Ah, hell. It was all for the best.

Gloomily, he fished out the key Dixie had given him and unlocked the door to the guesthouse. But he nearly stumbled when his toe connected with something unexpected.

A manila envelope, thick and menacing, lay on the

ground. Vaughn picked it up, saw his name scrawled in black marker. Inside the house, he tossed the envelope on the table and poured himself a drink. His luggage still sat at the foot of the stairs.

The master suite was on the top floor. A second, smaller bedroom was tucked away at the back of the main level. Because Dixie had saved the entire place for him, he wouldn't have to bother making small talk with any additional guests.

He was damned glad. Exhaustion went bone deep. Sometimes he wondered why he worked so hard. He'd already made more money than he could spend in a lifetime. Yet still, he had to accumulate more. It was the Blackwood way.

After finishing his scotch, he carried his bags upstairs. Then, unable to help himself, he went back down the stairs and picked up the envelope. Inside was a copy of his father's will. He'd never actually read the damn thing—or even heard it read, come to think of it. At the reading of the will, Kace LeBlanc, Buck's lawyer, had cut straight to the heart of it and told them all, flat out, that Miranda had gotten everything. But the document in Vaughn's hands now was conveniently folded back to a page that addressed him personally.

He sat down hard, felt his stomach pitch and began to read.

Dear Vaughn,

If you're reading this, you're probably pissed that I didn't leave you anything. The truth is, of all my progeny, you're probably the most like me.

You love the open road—not being constrained by anyone's expectations. You have a keen business sense, and you're a bit of a renegade. You don't want to settle down.

Unfortunately, all those characteristics make you a bad risk when it comes to relationships. I suffered the same weaknesses, and I ended up alone and lonely. Does that admission surprise you? I learned my lessons the hard way. I'm dying now with no one at my side to hold my hand.

So, I'm not leaving you any money. I'm hoping this letter from beyond the grave will convince you that the one thing you lack is the love of a good woman. I had two, and I lost them both.

Be angry with me if you must, but try to learn from my mistakes. Miranda will be the arbiter of what comes next. I've asked her to watch over my children and decide when and if each of you has matured enough to make good lives for yourselves.

I do love you, son. Don't be afraid to change.
Dad

Vaughn cursed and tossed the sheaf of papers aside. What a load of crap. This was why he had stayed far away from all the lawyer shenanigans.

Who had dropped off such a bombshell? Dixie? Surely not. She was more inclined to face problems head-on.

Vaughn was too jumpy and irritated to sleep, even though the hour was late. Instead, he changed into shorts and athletic shoes and left the house to outrun his demons.

The ranch was dark and quiet and mostly peaceful. Periodically, a lowing moo broke the silence. It was probably foolhardy to run in the dark, risking a broken ankle. But he was angry and upset and, though he was loath to admit it, hurt.

Maybe most men would be pleased to hear they were like their fathers. Not Vaughn. His dad had alienated his mother. Then married a woman young enough to be his child. Divorced her, too. At the end, he'd succumbed to cancer with no close family member at his side.

Vaughn ran faster, harder. He wasn't like his father. He wasn't. Maybe he was a loner, and maybe he liked keeping his emotions under control. Nothing wrong with that. It didn't matter what his father or *anyone* thought of him.

He lived by a set of rules that made sense. He was charitably generous, and he had a brother and a sister he cared about. His life was perfect.

Three

After a restless night, Vaughn sent Dixie a text to see if she would join him for coffee. Half an hour later, she showed up carrying a freshly baked coffee cake that smelled of cinnamon and culinary delight. He inhaled deeply. "Did you make this?"

She reached into a cabinet for plates and forks. "I could have, but I didn't. I have a new cook who enjoys reproducing our family recipes. I'm paying her a ridiculous salary so she won't leave me."

"Stick with that plan," he said, swallowing his first bite. "This is amazing."

Dixie joined him, and they ate their impromptu breakfast in harmony. When the last crumbs were gone, she eyed him wryly. "You haven't even been home twenty-four hours. What's wrong, Vaughn? You're so tense, you're giving *me* a headache."

He shrugged and pulled the sheaf of papers from underneath a stack of magazines. "I found this on the doorstep when I got home last night."

Dixie glanced at it. "Ah."

"That's all you have to say?"

"I didn't leave it there," she said. "Though I have seen it. Both Kellan and Sophie have copies."

"If it wasn't you, then who?"

"Probably Miranda. She knows you don't like her, so she wouldn't have wanted to make waves."

"Yet she's sticking her nose in my business." Vaughn's mood teetered between resigned and angry.

"If it was her, then she was just trying to carry out the terms of your father's will. Cut her a break."

"Forgive me if I'm not feeling particularly sympathetic toward Miranda right now." He stabbed his finger at the paragraphs that had given him a sleepless night. "Do *you* think I'm like my father?"

Dixie hesitated. Long enough to give him heartburn. His surrogate mother was honest to a fault.

She shook her head slowly. "You're *not* your father, Vaughn. But you do share some of his traits."

"Like what?"

"You've never learned how to open yourself up to other people. Even your brother and sister have a hard time knowing you."

"They said that?" He was startled and chagrined.

"Not in so many words. But we all worry about you, Vaughn. You're like a superhero with deep psychological wounds. You wear the cape or the mask, or you simply hide from the world. It's not healthy. I want more for you."

"I think you have a wonderfully caring heart, Dixie, and I'm glad you love me enough to worry about me. But if you're thinking that I need some big love story in order to be happy, think again. Just because Kellan and Sophie have wallowed in romance lately doesn't mean I will. I'm here for the wedding. That's it."

"Fair enough." She stood and gathered the dishes. "How was Sophie last night?"

The obvious change in subjects relieved him. "I thought I was just dropping by for a casual visit. But you know Sophie. There was a party underway. I had a few minutes with her and Kellan. Met Nigel. It was...nice."

He couldn't quite bring himself to mention Brie or that he was seeing her again this afternoon. Dixie would jump to conclusions, but there was nowhere to jump. Nowhere at all.

Brie closed the office for the lunch break and handed off the keys to her brand-new partner. Dr. Brody had been a veterinarian in Royal for over four decades. Since his retirement, he'd been at loose ends. When Brie had asked if he'd be willing to cover for her occasionally, Dr. Brody jumped at the chance.

He was thin and stooped, but his mind was as sharp as ever. Plus, he had a wealth of experience that could only enhance Brie's fledgling practice. It was the perfect solution for both of them.

Brie scooted home as quickly as she could and relieved the babysitter. Danika was already down for her nap. Brie missed her daughter fiercely when she was at work, but Brie was their sole financial support. No matter how much she would have loved to be a stay-at-home mom for a few years, it wasn't in the cards.

She eased open the bedroom door and slipped inside to watch her baby sleep. Not really a baby anymore. Danika would be two very soon. Where had the time gone?

Her daughter's hair was pale blond like Brie's. But the little girl had her father's vivid green eyes. Anyone looking closely could deduce the truth easily.

Brie had realized when she returned to Royal that she would have to face Vaughn sooner or later. He didn't live here anymore, but with his sister getting married, of course he was going to come home for a visit.

It might have been possible to avoid a confrontation for a week or ten days—long enough for him to leave town again. But Brie had known for some time now that she needed to make a concerted effort to connect father and daughter.

Vaughn didn't want family ties or obligations. That was fine. His choice. Still, Brie had to tell him the truth.

This move back to Royal was fraught with possibilities for happiness or for heartache, but Brie was convinced it was what was best for her little family. Brie wanted Danika to grow up in the wonderful town where she had spent her own childhood. Though Brie's parents had relocated to south Florida for their retirement, Royal would always be home. She wanted that sense of belonging for her daughter.

While Danika was still napping, Brie carried the baby monitor to the bathroom so she could shower and change. When her hair was dry and her light makeup redone, she chose black dress pants and a crimson silk blouse that lifted her spirits while suiting the weather. Royal was on the cusp of a mild winter and an early spring. Dressy black sandals gave her a couple of extra inches and completed her outfit.

Danika stirred just as her mother was ready. After a snack of applesauce and goldfish crackers, Brie dressed her daughter in a knee-length dress with short sleeves. The fabric was pale blue gingham. The white band of smocking across the upper chest incorporated a cute pattern of yellow ducks chasing brown bunnies.

Danika squirmed. The child's boundless energy didn't take well to hair brushing.

"Easy, baby," Brie said, expertly catching up the fine silky-blond strands into two small pigtails and adding blue bows. "Mommy's almost done."

Danika giggled when Brie lifted her little skirt and tickled her bare tummy. The baby had been wearing tights all winter, but today was balmy, so Brie put the child in a diaper and sandals and nothing else but her dress.

At last, both she and her daughter were ready to go. Brie had skipped lunch. Her stomach was in knots. Anxiety. Tension.

She was doing the right thing. No question.

But how would Vaughn react?

By the time Brie strapped Danika into her car seat, and they were headed toward Magnolia Acres, her forehead was damp and her hands were almost too shaky to drive.

She hadn't been this nervous since the day she sat in a doctor's office and heard the news that she was going to be a mother. She'd been all alone in a little suburb outside Houston.

After quitting her job at Blackwood Hollow she had fled Royal. Though Vaughn lived in Fort Worth, he came back and forth to Royal frequently. Their breakup had been ugly—too ugly for her to be comfortable with the idea of seeing him again. She'd been convinced that she had no choice but to leave Royal and start over.

Just as she was reliving her past, a car ran a stop sign and nearly clipped her bumper. Brie took a deep breath, sat up straight and concentrated on her driving. This looming confrontation was like ripping off a Band-Aid. The anticipation was always worse than the real event. Hopefully…

Besides, Vaughn wouldn't want anything more than a cursory relationship with little Danika. He might offer to write a check for child support. Brie would decline, and her responsibility to inform him would be over.

By the time she reached Magnolia Acres, her pulse was racing. Fortunately, Danika played happily with books in the back seat. She already spoke multiple words and short sentences and was picking up additional language skills every day.

Would Vaughn be impressed with his daughter? Or was fatherhood going to be nothing more than an inconvenience to him? Brie braced herself for the fact that he might simply be uninterested.

That would be the worst blow of all…

She bypassed the turn to the main house and headed for the guest quarters. The clock on the dash read three minutes before two. A rental car in the driveway told her that Vaughn had returned from his earlier plans with his sister.

After checking her reflection in the visor mirror and smoothing her hair, she got out and freed Danika from her car seat. “Showtime, sweet baby. Please be on your best behavior.” The child might not understand the seriousness of the situation, but hopefully she would be in her usual good mood.

Brie balanced her daughter on her hip, hefting the bag against her other side. The diaper bag went everywhere with them. It held toys and snacks and extra clothing, and it was easy to tuck her small purse inside. She didn’t relish arriving on Vaughn’s doorstep burdened down with the huge navy-and-white tote, but it wouldn’t be smart to leave it.

Was Vaughn watching them out the window? A trickle of sweat rolled down Brie’s spine. Her mouth was so dry she wondered if she would be able to speak.

She had rehearsed this speech a hundred times over the past two years. Now that the moment had come, her mind was blank.

At the door, she set down the diaper bag and cuddled Danika for moral support. Then she rang the bell.

Vaughn answered almost immediately. He was wearing dark khakis with a cream dress shirt and a fashionable tie, navy with tiny gold medallions. His navy sport coat looked wildly expensive.

"Hello, Vaughn." She spoke first, because his gaze had skidded over Brie and locked on the baby.

When Vaughn didn't say anything, her heartbeat lurched and thudded wildly. "This is Danika. Your daughter. I call her Nika for short."

Still, he was silent. As she watched anxiously, every ounce of color drained from his face, only to be replaced with two dark slashes of red on his cheekbones. She saw his Adam's apple flex visibly as he swallowed.

For a second, his incredulous gaze snapped back to meet Brie's, but then immediately he focused on Danika again. He didn't reach for the little girl. He didn't move. He simply stared.

At last, when the silent standoff seemed as if it would never end, he shot a piercing glance at Brie. An angry, in fact furious, stare. "You didn't think I had the right to know?"

"Whoa, whoa, back up the truck," Brie hissed, trying not to upset her daughter. "I *tried* to tell you. Several times. But apparently, you changed cell service providers, and I wasn't one of the chosen few you notified."

A flicker in his expression told her he remembered. "We had a data breach at work. The tech guys started all my team over from scratch with new phones. But you could have called the office. The main line. That number was no secret, Brie."

"I did," she insisted. "At least half a dozen times. Twice, I even got through to your administrative assistant. Do you have any idea how humiliating that was? Begging her to connect me to your line. I told her it was a personal matter. But apparently you've trained her to be very efficient when it comes to protecting your privacy."

"Well, hell..."

"Yeah. Tell me about it."

He seemed at a loss for words now. The situation was so novel—Vaughn Blackwood not knowing what to say—it was as if time stood still. Finally, he stepped back. "You should come in," he muttered. "She has such fair skin. Don't want her to get sunburned."

As Brie leaned down to grab the bag, Vaughn intervened. "I've got it. You hang on to her."

"Okay. Thanks."

Brie had been inside Dixie's guesthouse a time or two. She found herself fiercely glad that she and Vaughn were going to have this conversation on neutral ground. A lot was at stake.

"This place isn't childproofed," he said, looking around the room, his expression still half-dazed.

"I'll watch her. She'll be fine. Maybe you and I could sit on the sofa. That way she can play at the coffee table. I'll need the diaper bag, though."

When she said the word *diaper*, she was pretty sure Vaughn's eyes glazed over again. Brie took out a small set of colorful stacking cups, Danika's favorite soft baby doll and a sippy cup of water.

With interesting distractions, the little girl was happy to stand at the table while her mother sat down opposite the strange man. Now they mimicked a real family—the two grown-ups on either end of the sofa and the child in the middle.

Vaughn raked a hand through his hair, laughing

softly, though without any real humor. "I thought you wanted to borrow money."

Brie's eyes widened. "Why would I want money?"

"For the new veterinary practice?"

The way one of his eyebrows went up reminded her of a dozen arguments they'd had over the year and a half they had dated. With Brie working at his father's ranch and Vaughn based mainly in the Dallas/Forth Worth area, their affair had been full of obstacles from the beginning. Brie had been willing to fight her way past all of them—at least at first. Back when she'd thought there might be a future for them together.

The first time they made love, Vaughn had spread a quilt in the hayloft and coaxed her into spending most of the night with him. It had been intimate and wildly romantic. Too bad it had all been for show.

"I don't need your money," she said, perhaps a little too sharply. "My parents invested a modest sum in my practice, and I qualified for a small business loan. The clinic is doing fine."

His body language was guarded, arms folded over his broad, masculine chest. "Then why are you here?"

She gaped at him. "Seriously? I'm here so you can meet your daughter. Is that so odd? I know this whole parenthood gig probably means less than nothing to you, but a healthy child benefits from having two parents. I don't want her waking up one day and hating me because I never told her who you were."

"So this is really about *you* and not Danika. Certainly not me."

"God, you're a sanctimonious jerk. Some things

never change." She inhaled sharply, reining in her temper and reminding herself she didn't want to upset Nika. "I don't need or expect anything from you, Vaughn Blackwood. But my baby girl carries no blame here. If she wants a daddy, I'm going to make sure she knows who he is...even if he's an absent parent."

"I see."

"You can deny paternity. If you wish. But a court of law would find in favor of your daughter. Look at her eyes, Vaughn. She's yours. Through and through. If we're lucky, maybe she won't have inherited your stubborn, bullheaded need to push everyone away so you can always be in control."

Four

Vaughn's hands were cold. His insides were a mish-mash of anger and incredulity.

In control? He would have laughed wildly if the situation had been less fraught. He'd never felt less in control during his entire adult life.

One minute he'd been a dutiful brother showing up for his sister's wedding. The next he'd been blindsided by the woman and the past he had put behind him.

He stared at the child, searching for something, anything to tell him she was his. Brie was right. The eyes were a dead giveaway. Besides, he knew Brie. She wouldn't lie about something like this.

"How old is she?" he demanded.

"Almost two. Her birthday is coming up. You can do the math. I didn't know I was pregnant when I left

Royal. By the time I found out, I was working in Houston. At first I wasn't going to tell you at all, because you'd been so adamant about not wanting ties. But after a few weeks, my conscience kicked in, and I felt I had to share the truth. By then, it was too late. I couldn't reach you by phone."

"You could have come in person," he said stubbornly, still wanting to play the injured party.

"No. We were done. I wasn't going to crawl to you and beg for support, either financial or emotional."

In Brie's eyes, he saw the pain and trauma she had experienced since they parted. But he also saw her love for her daughter. *Their* daughter. He pressed two fingers to his forehead. "What have you told her about me?"

Brie shrugged. "Nothing yet."

He reached out a hand and touched the child's hair. It was silky and soft, though not as thick as her mother's. "Hello," he said quietly.

Danika sidled closer to Brie and put her thumb in her mouth, her eyes wide.

"It's okay, sweetie." Brie petted her. "Mr. V is our friend."

Vaughn raised an eyebrow? "Mr. V?"

"*Vaughn* is not easy for a toddler to say, though my daughter *is* super verbal. She can already name most of her alphabet letters—even if they're out of order."

"Why not *Daddy*?" He saw the flash of alarm that flitted across Brie's expressive sky-blue eyes.

"I don't think that's wise," she said quietly. "Not yet. No sense in confusing her with something that may be temporary."

He clenched his jaw, battling a host of conflicting emotions. "I want to see her."

"See her?" Brie's puzzlement was evident. "She's right in front of you."

"I want to see her while I'm here," he said, clarifying the notion that even now seemed foreign to him. "I want to spend time with her."

Brie's protective body language wasn't hard to read. She curled an arm around her daughter's small waist, pulling the girl against her legs. "You told me you weren't going to have much free time while you're in Royal," she snapped, her expression stormy now.

Vaughn shook his head, smiling ruefully. "You have the damnedest way of throwing my words back in my face, don't you?"

His humor seemed to ease something in Brie. She didn't turn warm, but she seemed less defensive. Now she was just sad and wary. "I'll be honest, Vaughn," she said quietly. "My hope is that I'll eventually fall in love with a man who will want to adopt Nika. That would be best for all of us. I don't really want her to get attached to you."

Vaughn took the hit stoically, at least on the outside. How could he complain about Brie's assumptions when he himself had shown absolutely zero interest in settling down?

He'd had a crappy example for a father. If genetics were any indication, Vaughn was probably more like the old man than he cared to admit. But when he looked at this tiny little girl, something cracked inside his heart. Something ached. Something hurt like hell.

He and Brie had created this quiet, precious child. Whether he wanted it or not, fatherhood had come knocking. Quite literally.

"Will she let me hold her?"

Brie gnawed her lip. "Maybe not today. But soon. She'll warm up to you if you play with her."

"Play?" The word was not in his repertoire, not in this innocent context.

"You know. Help her build a tower. Talk to her doll. Anything."

He sure as hell wasn't going to play ventriloquist with the doll. Not with Brie watching. Instead, he picked up a blue cup and an orange cup and fit them together. "Will you give me the red one?" he asked, smiling at the little girl whose eyes matched the ones Vaughn saw in the mirror every morning.

Danika wriggled free from her mother's embrace and took a step in his direction. She studied the cups solemnly, then picked up the one he had requested. "Red," she said proudly, handing it to him.

Vaughn added it to the top of the tower, his throat tight. "Good job," he croaked. He'd never given much thought to replicating his DNA…to passing on a living legacy for another generation.

Perhaps he was overreacting. He wasn't a sentimental man. Just because a tiny sprite of a girl carried his genes didn't make him a father. Not really. He knew better than anyone that parenting was more than a onetime sperm donation. Buck Blackwood had taught him that.

Vaughn shifted his attention to Brie. She'd been watching the brief exchange between father and daughter with pained, cautious interest. If he was reading her correctly, she was torn. Brie wanted him to care about his daughter, but at the same time, she didn't want to make room for him in the child's life.

"Thank you for bringing her," he said. He wanted to do more, to say more, but he was still in shock. This news wouldn't be absorbed in a day or even a week. He had a baby—a toddler now. Somehow he had to figure this out. Could he bear to spend the rest of his life knowing that somewhere in Texas another man was sleeping with Brie and parenting Vaughn's baby?

He stood up abruptly, startling Danika. The child looked up at him towering over her, and her bottom lip trembled. "Mama," she said tearfully.

Brie scooped her daughter and stood, as well. "We should go," she said.

He stared at the two females. Now that the initial shock had worn off, he was able to focus on the woman, not the baby. "I do appreciate you coming. Thank you for being honest with me. And..." Would it be weird to say that motherhood suited her? Because it did. She looked good. Really good. Stunning, in fact. Her crimson top flattered her pale, creamy skin. Despite the many hours she had spent outside as a ranch hand at Blackwood Hollow, her complexion was flawless. "I'm glad to see you doing so well," he finished, feeling awkward.

Brie gave him a small smile, almost reluctantly, as pink tinged her cheeks. "You, too, Vaughn. I've read several articles about your company. You've accomplished a lot for your age. Your father must have been really proud of you."

He shook his head slowly. "Nope. Not even close. You remember him, surely. I don't think he cared about anyone but himself."

"That's pretty harsh."

"But accurate."

Brie stroked her daughter's hair. Something about that slow, tender motion mesmerized Vaughn. For a split second, he flashed back to being in bed with Brie, sated and happy, while she stroked his chest with that same, gentle touch.

The memory took his breath. His body hardened in an instant. Lust and passion roared in his veins, as if some ancient lock had been broken, some wild, destructive spirit set free.

He trembled with wanting her. But he couldn't seduce Brie for the hell of it, even if she was willing. There was another person in the mix now. Small but significant.

"I'd like to visit her at your house," he said. "Do you object?"

After a long, fraught moment, Brie shook her head. "No. That's fine. If you're free tomorrow night, you could have dinner with us and help with bedtime."

His libido revved again. Everyone knew what mommies and daddies did when the kids were finally in bed. "What time?"

"Five thirtyish?"

His eyes widened. He hadn't dined that early in years. But then again, an early dinner and the baby's early bedtime meant plenty of extra opportunity for Vaughn to hash things out with Brie.

He pulled a business card from his wallet. "Text me your address. I'll be there," he said.

After Brie gathered Danika's toys and snacks and said a stilted goodbye, Vaughn watched the small car disappear down the driveway. He exhaled. Had he been holding his breath? Trying to keep himself in check? The past half hour had winded him emotionally.

Suddenly, he needed to talk to someone. Though he preferred keeping his own counsel as a rule, his world had been knocked awry. Sophie would be the perfect confidante as long as she didn't have another social event right now.

Vaughn drove to his sister's house in Pine Valley on autopilot. It was a relief to see the driveway empty, indicating that there was no shower or bridal tea or any other nonsense going on.

Nigel Townshend opened the door. The Englishman stepped back and ushered Vaughn into the foyer. "Hello, Vaughn." He glanced at his watch. "Sophie is resting, but it's time for her to be up. Let me go get her."

"Is she ill?" Vaughn felt mildly alarmed. His sister was always bubbly and energetic.

"No, just tired." Nigel grimaced. "The wedding preparations have been nonstop. And to be honest, damned stressful at times. She hasn't been sleeping."

"Ah. Makes sense." Vaughn shoved his hands in his pockets and leaned against the door. "I realize we don't know each other well. Or at all, really. But I want you to know how glad I am that she found you. My sister deserves the best life has to offer. If you ever hurt her, I'll neuter you."

Nigel grinned. "Duly noted." He waved a hand. "Make yourself at home. She'll be down in a minute."

Vaughn wandered into the elegant living room and paced. Sophie had redecorated since last year. Though the decor was sophisticated, the furniture looked comfortable. Unfortunately, Vaughn was too wired to sit.

When Sophie appeared, Nigel wasn't with her. The other man was sharp. He must have recognized Vaughn's unspoken urgency.

Sophie yawned and shoveled her hair from her face. "Sorry," she said. "I'm not usually this lazy. The party lasted pretty late. I'm paying for the indulgence."

He kissed her cheek and led her to the sofa, but when Sophie sat, Vaughn couldn't. He resumed pacing the length of the room twice and then stopped to stare at her. "I have news," he said. "Brace yourself."

Sophie's eyes widened. "Okay. What is it?"

Somehow, his throat closed up. It was almost impossible to force the words from his lips. "I have a daughter. Brie told me today. I'm a father."

His sister's smile was sweet. Compassionate. "Then my guess was right. When I first saw Brie in town with her little girl, I wondered if the baby was yours. Why did she wait so long to tell you?"

"It's complicated." He jingled the keys in his pocket, his body rigid with nervous energy. "I don't know what to do. I don't have room in my schedule for a kid. I'm a workaholic. You know that. The whole reason Brie and I broke up was because she wanted a normal family. A simple, uncomplicated life. That's not something I can give." He pretended to study a picture on the wall. Would his sister judge him for his shortcomings? Was he a disappointment to her?

Sophie stood and hugged him from behind, resting her cheek on his back. "Don't be afraid to change."

He stiffened. Sophie had read the letter from his father, too. "I'm not afraid," he said automatically. "Maybe I just don't *want* to change."

"You have this persona you show the world, Vaughn, but I know better. My brother is sweet and honorable and has a huge heart."

He turned around and grinned. "You take that back. Where would I be if word got out that the head of Blackwood Energy Corporation had a heart? My reputation would be shot."

"Very funny." She paused and cocked her head. "So where does Brielle fit into all this?"

"She's my child's mother—nothing more. At this point she has to agree to my spending time with Danika, but that's it."

"And you really believe that?"

"Brie and I were over a long time ago. I know exactly what she thinks of me, and it isn't good."

"I'm more concerned about what you think of her."

Sophie's probing irritated him, but he had opened himself up to this personal intrusion by coming to his sister for advice. "Brie is a lovely, capable, independent woman. She doesn't want or expect anything from me. The fact that she's the mother of my child complicates things, but I can handle it."

"Have you thought about the fact that your daughter, your flesh and blood, has been disinherited?"

"Of course I have…from the moment I found out about the baby. I know I said I wasn't interested in being part of the suit with you and Kellan to challenge the will, but things have changed now. I'm going to confront Miranda and demand that Danika receive her fair share—my share."

"I'm afraid you've missed your opportunity," Sophie said. "Miranda flew back to New York this morning. The Twitter feed for *Secret Lives of NYC Ex-Wives* was all over it."

Vaughn snorted. "Please tell me you're not an actual fan of that stupid show."

"It's not stupid. Don't be so narrow-minded."

"If it's actually any good, then I can't believe Miranda is involved."

"Maybe she thinks it's good press for her company and her charity. Besides, it's harmless fun."

"Nothing about Miranda Dupree is harmless."

Sophie shook her head slowly. "That's your biggest weakness, Vaughn Blackwood. You get locked on an idea and you don't want to let go, even when you're wrong."

Five

As soon as Vaughn left, Sophie grabbed her keys and purse and headed out the door.

Nigel called after her. "Where are you going?"

She waved at her gorgeous English hunk of a fiancé. "Running an errand. Won't be long."

Guilt gnawed at her, but she kept driving. If she had asked Nigel's opinion, or even Vaughn's, they both would have said the same thing. *Don't rock the boat. It's not your business. Stay out of it, Sophie.*

Pooh. Men never understood the really important things in life until you beat them over the head with them. Sophie was an *aunt*! She wasn't going to sit on this news for a single minute longer.

It wasn't like she and Brielle were strangers. They weren't what you would call bosom buddies, but Royal was a small place—especially when someone was working on your father's ranch. When Vaughn and Brie had been dating, Sophie had interacted with her brother's girlfriend on a fairly regular basis.

The breakup and Brie's subsequent move had put an end to that budding female friendship. But today was a new day.

Sophie parked in front of the neat blue-and-white cottage Brie had been renting since her return to Royal. It was small but charming. When Sophie rang the doorbell, Brie answered almost immediately, the baby on her hip.

"Sophie." Brie's eyes widened. "What a surprise."

Sophie couldn't help herself. She reached out and touched the child's pale blond hair. "Vaughn told me," she muttered.

"He did? I wasn't even sure he had decided to claim her."

"How could he not? Look at those eyes. I've seen you and the baby around town and guessed she might be a Blackwood, but I was never close enough to see the eyes. That moss-green color is not common, you know."

"I do know. Would you like to come in?"

"Yes, please. She's gorgeous, Brie."

"Thank you. Sorry for the mess. I just fed her a grilled cheese, and I haven't had time to clean up the kitchen."

"Don't be silly. I'm family. Will she let me hold her?"

"You can try."

Sophie summoned her most winsome smile. "Hi, baby girl. I'm your aunt Sophie. Would you like to play with my necklace?" The chunky silver and cobalt beads were just the right size to fascinate a tiny child.

Danika held out her arms, and Sophie scooped her close, her heart melting. "You're so lucky, Brie. She's an angel."

Brie laughed and began loading the dishwasher. "Most of the time." She paused. "Does Vaughn know you're here?"

"Oh no. I'm sure he wouldn't approve. My dear brother likes to keep all the parts of his life in neat little boxes."

"Ouch." Brie looked chagrined.

"Sorry. I don't mean to be rude. But you must know how he is."

"I threw him a curve today. A huge one. I'm sure he's struggling with the information."

"You could say that."

Brie paled. "Is he super upset?"

"No. I'd call him flummoxed. I don't think he knows *how* to react."

"To be clear, I didn't ask him for anything. I just thought he should know. One day Nika may want to find out who he is."

"You're assuming Vaughn won't be around as an active part of her life."

"I am, yes. He's made no secret of the fact that he doesn't want to be a father."

"But now he is one. Things change. People change."

Brie folded her arms across her waist and leaned against the counter. "I'm not sure they do. Vaughn is a stubborn Texas male and set in his ways."

"Give him a chance, Brielle. He may surprise you."

"Maybe."

"You don't want him to change?"

"It's not that. I don't want my daughter to become a pawn in the Blackwood family dynamics. No offense, but you rich people have some serious issues."

Sophie laughed. "Fair enough." She snuggled Nika, giving her a theatrically loud kiss on the cheek, making the child giggle. "I have a favor to ask, Brie. It's very important."

Brie's eyes rounded. "Oh?"

"I've wanted all along to have a flower girl in my wedding. But everybody told me kids are too unpredictable. That they would be an extra layer of complication I didn't need."

"I won't argue with that. I've seen several weddings where tiny ring bearers and flower girls dissolved into tantrums."

"I don't care. I want my niece to walk down the aisle in front of me."

Brie winced. "Oh gosh, Sophie. I don't think that's a good idea at all. The wedding is almost here, and Vaughn would have a coronary. No matter what he decides about being part of Danika's life, I'm darned sure he doesn't want to parade her in front of everyone he knows at the wedding."

"We don't have to announce that she's my niece. You and I are friends. Maybe I just asked you because you have a sweet little girl exactly the right age."

"I'm beginning to see that Vaughn's stubborn streak is genetic."

"Please say yes. I'll take care of her dress and everything. Size two?"

"Are you sure, Sophie? I would feel terrible if my baby ruined your wedding."

"Can't happen. The only thing that could ruin my day is if Nigel changed his mind. And that's not in the cards." She smiled smugly. "He adores me."

Brie grinned, though it looked a little forced. "Lucky you."

By the time Sophie departed and Brie got Danika in bed and to sleep, Brie was exhausted. The highly emotional day had left her with a host of conflicted feelings. While she was glad Vaughn wasn't averse to knowing his daughter, this new relationship would put Brie in dangerous territory.

It was one thing for a single woman to have a crazy fling with a gorgeous millionaire. But Brie was a mother now. She had responsibilities. Even if her libido went crazy when Vaughn was nearby, she had to keep her priorities straight.

Still, all the lectures in the world couldn't erase her excitement and anticipation about the following evening. She slept restlessly and barely made it to work on time the next morning. Fortunately, her schedule was tight. Her furry patients and their owners were demanding.

Though she loved what she did, the day felt like it was about a million hours long. By the time she made it home, she had only forty-five minutes to get ready. She had put a roast in the slow cooker that morning along with carrots and potatoes. It was a simple meal for a man accustomed only to the best, but Danika liked it, and that was all that mattered.

Since the babysitter was still on the clock, Brie was able to grab a quick shower and change into jeans and a soft, navy V-neck cotton sweater. She added small pearl stud earrings that had been a twenty-first-birthday present from her parents along with a dainty silver chain that supported a third pearl only slightly larger than the others.

It was a far more casual outfit than the one she had worn to take Danika to meet her father. Adding the jewelry dressed it up enough to be presentable for an evening at home…with the man who had gotten her pregnant.

Unbidden, her mind went back to all those long, lonely months before Nika was born. Brie had yearned for Vaughn so badly she thought her heart would break. The only way she had disciplined herself was to repeat over and over that the Vaughn she *wanted* him to be was not the real one. And the man he was would never be willing to change—certainly not just to please her.

She needed a lover in her life who was devoted to her and willing to do anything to make the relationship work. Vaughn was virile and incredibly masculine and phenomenally talented in bed, but he didn't *need* anyone.

That was ultimately why Brie had walked away. Long before she knew she was going to have a child, she recognized that sooner or later, Vaughn Blackwood would break her heart.

Though *Brie* had been the one to leave, the breakup was no less painful. After she left Royal, she had planned to start dating immediately…to quickly wipe the memories of Vaughn from her head and her heart.

The plan was flawed from the beginning. She found out she was pregnant, and suddenly, Vaughn was a part of her in a way she could never erase. When the baby was born, the invisible intimacy grew more intense.

All those nights Brie nursed Nika at her breast, her mind was free to wander. In her fantasies, Vaughn was there in the bed beside her, his gaze warm and loving as he stroked his daughter's downy head…as he gently kissed Brie's cheek and told her how much he loved her.

Those daydreams, those fictional vignettes, kept Brie going. It probably wasn't healthy. But it was all she had.

With one last glance at her reflection in the bathroom mirror, she cataloged every bit of stress and excitement duking it out in her stomach. Why did Vaughn want to spend time with Danika? He'd made it very clear over the months he and Brie had dated that he was a free agent.

Maybe tonight was nothing more than simple curiosity.

When Brie made her way to the living room, the babysitter was standing beside the front door holding Nika and chatting with Vaughn. When the older woman said her goodbyes, Brie tensed. She wasn't sure how to play this.

Vaughn took the decision out of her hands. Casually, as though they hadn't been separated by two years and countless miles, he leaned forward, cupped her face in his big, warm hands and kissed her on the forehead. "Hello, Brie. I like what you've done with the house."

The affectionate greeting flustered her. She didn't trust his good humor.

"Thank you. I was lucky to find a suitable rental so close to my office."

Boring. Something about this reunion made her gauche and awkward. She felt as if this moment was some kind of test, and she was failing miserably.

She wanted to roll back the clock, fling her arms around Vaughn and kiss him until he was dizzy with wanting. What followed next would be good for both of them. For the moment, at least.

But that wasn't going to happen.

Swallowing her disappointment that Vaughn seemed far more calm about this shared meal than she was, she managed a smile. "Dinner's almost ready. Would you like to open the wine?"

"Of course. If you'll point me to the corkscrew and crystal, I'll do the honors."

Brie set Danika in a quiet corner of the kitchen and gave her a wooden spoon and a plastic mixing bowl. It was a combination guaranteed to keep the child happy for at least fifteen minutes.

Vaughn poured the merlot as promised and handed Brie a glass. "To surprises," he said, his expression enigmatic.

Her throat was tight, but she managed to swallow. "To surprises." She paused. "I don't mean to disrupt your life. I hope you know that. And hopefully, this won't create too many complications for you. It might be awkward if you lived here, but you don't."

She studied him while he sipped his wine, his gaze downcast as if he were studying the shine on his expensive Italian leather dress shoes. His dark slacks and pristine white shirt were topped with a tweedy sport coat that matched his thick brown hair.

And that square jaw. *Oh, lordy.* She remembered pressing kisses across Vaughn's face and along that gorgeous chin.

At the moment, he leaned casually against the cabinet, his long legs crossed at the ankle. He swirled his wine and studied the resultant pattern as if it held answers she couldn't give him.

Finally, he looked up. "I don't live here, that's true. But Royal is my home. And Danika is my child. I have some opinions on the matter, as it happens."

Brie stiffened. She heard the veiled threat clearly. Now that she had involved Vaughn, he wasn't going to quietly disappear. Questions hovered on her lips, but she restrained herself. It was almost impossible to win a battle of wits with Vaughn. With the full day she'd put in, she was physically tired—and all the fretting she'd done over this dinner had her emotionally exhausted. Needless to say, she was not at her best, not to mention the fact that she had a meal to get on the table.

"I'm sure you do," she muttered. "But Nika will start fussing if I don't feed her soon. When she's ready to eat, she's ready."

He nodded slowly. "Very well. My opinions will keep for the moment. What can I do to help?"

She shot him a startled glance. The Vaughn Blackwood she remembered rarely frequented the kitchen. He was the least domesticated man she knew.

Her skepticism must have been visible. His wry smile took him from handsome to heartbreaking. "Do I seem so incompetent to you, Brie?"

She weighed her words. "Not incompetent. More like uninterested. And that's fine," she said quickly. "I don't need any help with the meal. Just keep an eye on the baby, please."

She worked quickly. The small house didn't have a formal dining room. But the kitchen was fairly large and accommodated the slightly scarred oak table the landlord provided per the "mostly furnished" portion of her lease. Brie set out neutral place mats and the brightly colored Fiestaware that had been her grandmother's.

Soon, everything was on the table, including a spinach salad with warm bacon dressing and the yeast rolls she had purchased at a local bakery on her lunch break. She scooped up the baby, washed Nika's hands and popped her in her high chair.

Vaughn watched the entire exercise in silence, waiting to seat Brie. His innate courtesy brought him far too close. His warm breath brushed her cheek. "Are you comfortable?" he asked, scooting the chair an additional inch.

Brie squirmed inwardly. Was he joking? The last thing she wanted to do was eat dinner right now. He was too handsome, too tempting. Too everything…

Six

Vaughn wasn't comfortable, not in the least. He'd been half-hard since he walked in the front door and saw his ex-lover. He had vivid memories of making love to Brie, her beautiful body naked, wearing nothing but that single-pearl necklace.

Was the jewelry choice intentional? Was Brie trying to spark a reunion? It seemed unlikely. Despite that, she looked so damned sexy and seductive tonight, he could barely remember why they had argued and split up. Until his gaze landed on the toddler happily shoving mashed carrots and potatoes into her mouth.

Brie hadn't been kidding about the kid's appetite.

He hadn't thought he was hungry, but the aroma of roast beef and all the trimmings made his stomach growl. "I didn't know you were such a good cook," he said. Now that he thought about it, the two of them had never done anything so ordinary as enjoying dinner and a movie at home. When their affair was at its peak, he had wined and dined her at the finest restaurants around when he wasn't making love to her under the inky Texas night sky.

Then it was over.

Brie's smile seemed genuine. "Thanks. This is an easy meal. I try to feed her healthy stuff, but I'll admit I sometimes resort to chicken nuggets on days when I have to work late."

"You shouldn't have to work at all," he said. "She's my child. I can pay for her support entirely."

Now his dinner companion bristled visibly. "I *like* my job. Not more than my child, obviously. And I'll admit, it would be a luxury to stay at home with her. But being a vet is what I've trained for, what I've dreamed of since I was a kid. Moms can be moms and do other things, too. This is the twenty-first century, Vaughn. Try to keep up."

Her snappish response amused rather than insulted him. "I'm as evolved as the next man. But even you have to admit that money makes life easier."

Both of her eyebrows went up at the same moment. "*Even me?* What does that mean?"

He shrugged. "When we were dating, you didn't like me showering you with gifts. You said it made you feel weird. Like I was paying for your affections."

"I had a chip on my shoulder about your money. It's true." Her cheeks took on a rosy hue, making her look younger and more vulnerable. "I was a ranch hand on your father's property. Literally no one thought we were a good match. And they were right."

"Maybe they were, maybe they weren't. But we were talking about money. Regardless of what relationship I have with my daughter, my moral obligation is to support her financially. I certainly have the means. There's no reason the two of you should ever want for anything."

Brie's gaze narrowed. "You're forgetting how well I know you, Vaughn Blackwood. In that scenario, you'd be expecting me to do things *your* way as soon as I cashed the first check. You can set up a college fund for her. And we can talk about things like insurance. But Danika and I are fine."

"The offer stands," he said calmly. "Child support aside, there's a bigger angle to consider."

"Oh?"

"I want Nika to have every opportunity to receive what's due her when it comes to my father's holdings. I've said loudly that I don't care about my father's money, and that's true. Danika changes everything, though. Kellan and Sophie have already started a legal process to challenge the will. I wasn't planning to join them, but I won't disqualify myself if it means possibly securing Danika's future. Her university studies, a wedding one day. She's a Blackwood. She deserves to inherit a portion of her grandfather's estate."

Brie set her fork on her plate and stared at him. "I've never really thought of her as Buck's grandchild. That's odd, isn't it? I think of her as *my* baby and your daughter. It's been just the two of us, me and my little one.

Until Sophie showed up yesterday, I honestly hadn't realized that your siblings might care about her, too."

"Sophie came here?"

"Yes. She wants Danika to be a flower girl in the wedding. I told her it was your call. Sophie said even if you don't want to claim Nika just yet—or ever—she could simply say to anyone who asks that she and I are friends, and that I agreed to let Danika play a part in the festivities."

Vaughn frowned. Did his own sister think he would be such a moral coward as to hide the fact that he was Danika's father? "The child is mine. I'll do my duty by her, regardless. I won't let anyone say I've shirked my duty."

Brie wrinkled her nose. "Lovely."

"I'm sensing sarcasm."

"What do you expect?" Stormy blue eyes judged him and found him wanting. "The only reason I decided to tell you about Nika is that she may seek you out one day. Emotionally, if for no other reason. Little girls need their daddies. If nothing else, they should know who their daddies are."

"I thought you had plans to get married." It was a cheap shot under the circumstances, but he was in the midst of a battle.

Brie blinked and speared a carrot. She looked at it blankly as if she had forgotten they were all having dinner. "I do. I want to. But I can't guarantee I'll find someone."

Vaughn disagreed. Even if Brie and Danika were a package deal, it was a foregone conclusion that any number of men would want to wrangle a spot in Brie Gunderson's bed. Vaughn certainly had at one time. He'd been obsessed with her.

Echoes of that maddening physical insanity swirled in his gut. It had been sexual attraction back then, nothing more. And though the pheromones might still be the same, he and Brie were different people now.

The adults finished their dinner mostly in silence. Nika babbled constantly. Even Vaughn was beginning to pick out words and phrases. And while he was hardly an expert on toddlers, he thought her vocabulary was wider than he would have expected. She really was smart…he could already tell. Pride swelled in his chest. Totally ridiculous, of course. Even so, he was damn proud that he had fathered such a delightful child.

Without warning, the baby chortled and flung her arms wide, hitting Vaughn square in the chest with a blob of mushy carrots. For a split second, nothing happened. Danika's eyes opened wide, as if she realized she had broken some unspoken rule.

Brielle, on the other hand, burst out laughing. She laughed so hard her face turned red, and her cheeks were wet.

"I'm sorry," she gasped, trying to compose herself and failing miserably. "If you could see the look on your face…"

Vaughn stood and grabbed a paper towel, wetting it and dabbing the front of his shirt. "I'm glad you find me so entertaining," he muttered.

When he began unbuttoning his shirt, every trace of amusement fled from Brie's face. "What are you doing?" she asked. The last word came out as more of a gasp.

He unfastened his cuffs one at a time. "I thought it was obvious. I'm taking off my shirt so you can help me get the stain out. This one is brand-new, damn it. And it's one of my favorites."

Brie stood suddenly, almost knocking over her chair. "No, no, no," she sputtered. "Stop that." She shoved his hands away and tried to pull the sides of the shirt together. "It can't be your favorite, surely. It's nothing but a white shirt. I'll buy you another."

He'd been about to tug the tail of the shirt from his pants, but now he stopped. When Brie's fingers touched his skin, he froze as his erection came to life again. He swallowed. "Does my bare chest bother you that much, Brie?"

She was so close to him he could smell the tantalizing scent of her light perfume. Something with roses and magic and other things designed to make a man go mad with lust.

Her bottom lip trembled visibly. "Of course not," she said unconvincingly. "But I can't have a half-naked man wandering around my house."

"Why not?" He moved slowly, waiting to see if she would protest. But her gaze locked on his, and she leaned forward the slightest bit. He tugged her a few feet away, out of Nika's line of vision, and kissed Brie's chin, moved below her ear for another kiss. Then one cheek and the other.

Brie stood like a deer in the forest hoping a hunter won't notice its presence. Her chest was rising and falling so rapidly she might be in danger of hyperventilating. One of her hands gave up the battle to realign the sides of his shirt and instead flattened against the center of his rib cage.

"There's a baby here," she said. "I don't want her to see you like this." She stroked his collarbone slowly, clearly unaware that she was driving him crazy.

"Are you worried about *Nika* or you, Brie?"

Her mouth opened and shut. "You know the answer to that," she said wryly. "Kiss me, Vaughn."

He settled his lips over hers, groaning inwardly. God, she was sweet. His tongue stroked hers coaxingly, feeling and hearing the little catch in her breath.

Suddenly, the calendar rolled backward, dragging them toward a time when nothing had mattered but the physical pleasure they could find together. Brie was warm and soft in his arms. He shuddered hard, as if hit by an electric shock. The kiss went from sweet to carnal in a white-hot flash of heat.

Brie kissed him back. Unmistakably. Her arms linked around his neck. Her teeth nipped his bottom lip, then suckled it.

His knees threatened to buckle. He reached for the button on her jeans, intent on only one thing. He had to have her.

When his fingers brushed the downy skin of her belly, Brie screeched and jumped back, nearly falling. She covered her cheeks with her hands, her expression aghast. "Are you mad?" she whispered. "The baby."

Danika, in her total innocence, had no idea that the adults were contemplating doing naughty things on the kitchen table. Or at least *one* of the adults was. Vaughn's heart galloped like a Derby winner. "I forgot," he said. Then he winced when he heard the words aloud. What kind of parent *forgot his own kid*?

Brie backed away another few inches, her gaze not meeting his. "I have to bathe her and get her ready for bed. Make yourself comfortable in the living room. We can…talk when she's asleep. And please button your damn shirt."

The tiny pause before the word *talk* gave him hope. Was Brie thinking the same things he was thinking? "I can help bathe her," he said, wanting to hurry things along.

Brie shook her head. "No. She's slippery and small. You're not used to it…"

"How can I ever learn if I don't practice? I was pretty good at holding on to a football when I quarterbacked in college."

A wry smile twisted Brie's lips. "If you're comparing our little toddler to a piece of sporting equipment, I have a feeling you're not ready for the nighttime routine."

He winced. "Bad choice of words." Perhaps he needed to back off and give Brie some breathing room. That little *moment* between them had clearly rattled her. It sure as hell had rattled him.

He held up his hands. "Fine. But do I at least have permission to load the dishwasher?"

She looked uneasy. "I suppose so. But it's not necessary."

"I think I can handle it."

Brie scooped up her daughter, brushed what looked

like a pound of crumbs into the high chair and stripped the baby down to her diaper. Danika laughed and pulled her mother's hair.

Again, Brie gazed at Vaughn with hesitation. "Go," he said. "I've got this."

Moments later, he heard water running in the hall bathroom. The house was small. Sounds carried. The conversation between mother and daughter was strangely sweet. Completely ordinary, but tender and heartwarming.

As he went about his task on autopilot, he couldn't help thinking about all the nights like this he had missed. Anger stirred again, mixed with searing regret. No one was to blame for what had happened. That didn't make it any less painful.

Would anything have changed if he had known Brie was pregnant? It was a difficult question to answer. Two years ago he had spent a great deal of time pushing her away, making it clear that he wasn't interested in a serious or lasting relationship. He had told himself he was being honest. A straight shooter.

The truth wasn't so clear-cut. When Brie broke up with him and disappeared, he had been forced to face up to his own duplicity. Why had he let her go? And worse, why had he really gotten involved with her? Had he gone out with her initially to get in his father's face? To make the old man angry? One of the Blackwood heirs consorting with a ranch hand?

The fact that Vaughn couldn't say a definitive no made him ashamed. With most of the kitchen tidy, he made his way down the hall and leaned against the door frame of the bathroom. Brie was on her knees beside the tub trying to shampoo the baby's hair.

Danika was having none of it. She wriggled and squirmed and then howled when she got soap in her eyes. Brie shot him a glance over her shoulder. "Hand me that towel, will you?"

He reached for the white terry cloth with the yellow duck-face hood. "Is it always like this?"

After wiping the baby's eyes and rinsing the lather from her hair, Brie leaned down and picked up the wet, constantly-in-motion child and wrapped her in the towel. The dead lift made *Vaughn's* back hurt. And he wasn't even helping.

She nodded. "Usually. Nika loves playing in the bath with all her foam toys, but when I have to get serious with the soap, she's never happy about it."

Vaughn followed the two females into the nursery. The walls were pale green with thin yellow stripes. He wondered if the paint job had come with the house or if Brielle was one of those moms who was not a fan of all pink for girls all the time.

When the toddler was diapered and clad in soft one-piece pajamas, Brie sat her in the crib and handed her a teething ring.

"Whew," she said, fanning herself. "That exercise burns a lot of calories."

Vaughn stared at her, his heart pounding. "Your shirt is all wet," he said hoarsely. "I can see…"

Brie looked down at her chest. The red in her cheeks deepened. Though the navy fabric was not at all transparent, her puckered nipples were outlined beneath the soft cotton.

"I'm cold," she said. "I should change."

"You just told me in so many words that you were hot."

Her chin jutted, her eyes flashing. "And now I'm cold. What's your point?"

He took her wrist and reeled her in. "No point, beautiful mama. Except that you still want me, don't you?"

Seven

Brie could have pulled away. Vaughn's grip on her wrist was loose. But she went to him so easily, he must have thought she was sex starved. She would never tell him she hadn't had sex with anyone since he'd made her pregnant. That was too much ammunition for a man who was already shockingly arrogant.

He gripped a handful of her hair and tipped back her head so he could sink his teeth into her throat. "I want to strip you bare," he said roughly. "Your breasts are bigger. I can feel them. God, Brie, it's been an eternity since I've been inside you."

The gruff, carnally explicit words turned her into a shuddering mess. She was so desperate for him, her whole body trembled. Suddenly, they were racing toward a precipice she had sworn never to face again. This was madness, pure and simple.

Drawing on every ounce of strength she possessed, she pulled away and wiped her mouth. “Excuse me,” she said, her tone ridiculously formal. “I need to rock the baby to sleep.”

Vaughn was visibly shaken. He took several deep breaths and raked his hands through his hair. “I can do it,” he said gruffly. “I won’t drop her, I swear.”

She couldn’t read him. Not at all. Other than the lust. That was clear. And yet every time she redirected his focus to Nika, he jumped to help with the baby. Was he curious about this whole fatherhood thing? Was he testing the waters?

“Fine,” she said abruptly. “I’ll be in my bedroom if you need me for anything.”

One dark eyebrow went up. Green eyes sizzled with heated amusement. “What a lovely offer.”

“Not that, cocky man. You know what I mean.” She escaped before she could say something else stupid.

Grabbing a shirt from her dresser drawer, she hid in the bathroom to do the quick change. Even her bra was wet. When she removed it and didn’t bother to replace it with a dry one, she knew she was making a choice.

Who could blame her? She hadn’t felt a man’s touch on her body in almost three years. It had been so long she wasn’t sure she remembered what it was like to be a woman consumed with arousal.

When she was decently covered in a fresh shirt, she returned to her daughter’s room and lingered quietly in the doorway. Vaughn was reading the toddler a book.

Nika must have asked for it. Her eyes were heavy. She nestled trustingly against her father's chest.

A baby couldn't possibly know the truth, could she? Was there some instinctive connection Brie didn't understand? Was the power of blood strong enough to bind child to man?

Brie kept silent, loath to intrude on the scene. Vaughn wasn't entirely comfortable. She could see that. But he plodded on. As crazy as it sounded, his clumsy rendering of the story made Brie's heart turn over. At least he was trying.

When the story wound to an end and Vaughn closed the book, Brie stepped into the room. "I'll take her now. Why don't you go grab yourself a drink and relax?"

He nodded, his expression inscrutable. Moments later, Brie was alone with her daughter. Danika's body was limp, her breathing heavy. There was really nothing left to do but lay her in bed and tiptoe out of the room.

In the hallway, Brie leaned against the wall and put a hand to her heart, trying to still the wild thumping. Nothing was going to happen right now. Not until she made up her mind.

Vaughn was a gentleman to the core, despite his libido. He wouldn't force himself on her.

But what if the tables were turned?

She found him in the living room sprawled on one end of the sofa, his expression moody as he channel surfed. For safety's sake, she chose an armchair several feet away. "It's still early," she said. "I'm sure you have things to do. Thanks for dropping by. You're welcome any time."

He shot her a fulminating glare. “You don’t have to lay it on so thick, Brie. If you don’t want me here, I can take a hint.”

For a moment she thought she might have bruised his feelings, but that was absurd. “I don’t think it’s wise for us to be alone together.” There. That was plain enough.

He sat up straight and tossed the remote aside. “So because I noticed your nipples, you’re kicking me out?”

She crossed her arms over her chest. “Don’t be absurd. You wanted to spend time with your daughter. And you did. Now she’s asleep. End of story.”

His expression softened. “You’re not wearing a bra, Brielle, even though you were before you changed clothes. What is a man like me supposed to take from a thing like that?”

Chewing her lip, she stared anywhere but at him, feeling her face flame. “It was wet.”

“Ah. And you only own the one?”

He had her there. Why was she being such a coward? She wanted to have sex with him. When she’d omitted the bra, she thought she knew where the night would go. But she was allowed to change her mind. She didn’t want to get sucked into his masculine force field again. She couldn’t let herself be vulnerable to his charming, rakish ways.

“Fine,” she snapped. “I’m not wearing a bra. Big deal. Lots of women take their bras off when they get home from work.”

He rolled to his feet, all six feet plus of him. “Do you want me as much as I want you, Brie? You don’t have to be afraid to say it." The taunting tone in his voice lit her temper.

"I'm *not* scared of you, Vaughn Blackwood. Feel free to go."

The fact that she took two steps in his direction dampened her dismissal.

Vaughn's shirt still hung open. In fact, it barely clung to his shoulders. She could see almost every inch of his tanned, muscular, yummy-enough-to-lick chest.

The arrogance faded. His smile was kind now, alarmingly so. "I'm not going anywhere, sweet Brie. Not unless you walk over to that front door, unlock it and tell me—unequivocally—to leave. Are you going to do that?"

If he had been a jerk about it, she might have followed through on kicking him out. But he was letting her see how much he wanted to stay. That sincerity, in the end, tipped the scales.

She sighed. "It's only seven forty-five. Isn't that too early for hanky-panky?"

He chuckled. "I'd say it's about two and a half years too late. I've missed you in my bed, woman."

"We'll be in mine this time," she warned. "It's only a queen, and the mattress sucks."

"I think I can handle it."

"And we both agree this means nothing." Somehow, it was important to lay that out there.

"Whatever you say." He shrugged out of his shirt and tossed it aside.

Dear. Sweet. Lord. Gooseflesh broke out all over her

body. Erogenous zones she had forgotten about beat out a chorus of pulsing, erotic intent.

"I, uh..."

He grinned widely. "The Brie I remember didn't used to be so shy."

"I'm not shy," she protested. "I'm just not sure of the protocol for scratch-an-itch sex."

Without warning, he scooped her up in his arms and strode toward the hall. "Well, for one thing," he said, breathing a tiny bit harder than her weight should have warranted, "it doesn't usually get off to such a slow start."

She laid her head against his chest, feeling weepy for no particular reason, so she cracked a joke to lighten the mood. "As long as you get *me* off, big guy, I won't complain." This was what she had missed...what she wanted and needed. Laughter and verbal sparring with the man who had been such a pivotal part of her life.

But that relationship was over now. Whatever was left was so much less than what she had once hoped to have in a partner.

He kicked open her bedroom door and tossed her onto the center of the mattress. "Don't go anywhere." With impressive speed, he stripped out of his clothes. When he was bare-ass naked, she inhaled sharply. Vaughn Blackwood was one big, bad, gorgeous male.

His wicked smile made her squirm. As he sprawled onto the bed beside her, he began unfastening buttons and such.

Brie lay perfectly still, her fingers clenched in the covers. Every muscle in her body was rigid.

At one point, Vaughn stopped and looked at her with a little frown creasing the spot between his brows. "Brie? Are you sure this is what you want?"

She forced herself to relax. "Yes," she whispered. "Sorry. I'm just nervous."

He leaned over her on one elbow. "Why, sweet thing? It's like riding a bike." His droll comparison was meant to make her smile, but she was too tense.

"Bicycle crashes hurt. I don't want to get hurt again. I need you to know that I don't expect empty words or romantic gestures. All I want from you is an orgasm or two. So don't get the wrong impression. We're not picking up where we left off."

His frown deepened. "Are you finished?" he asked, his green-eyed gaze glacial.

"With what?"

"Reading me the fine print."

She had made him angry. Too bad. There had to be ground rules. Otherwise, having her baby's father back in her life would destroy Brie. They weren't playing house.

"I'm finished," she said.

He moved half on top of her with an audible groan. The man was fully aroused and ready to go.

So was Brie. Her body wept for him. The fact that she now had stretch marks and a stomach that was no longer taut and firm made her self-conscious for about thirty seconds. After that, Vaughn's voracious appetite told her more loudly than words that he wanted her exactly as she was.

He spread her thighs, poised to enter her.

"Wait," she cried. "Condoms?"

Vaughn seemed shocked. "You're not on birth control?"

"No. Single moms with full-time jobs don't have much time for extracurricular activities. Sorry. I wasn't expecting this."

His hunger for her blazed in his eyes, making her shiver. "Neither was I," he grumbled, "but I do have one condom in my wallet." He retrieved the protection and rolled it on.

The fleeting disappointment Brie felt at knowing this was a one-shot event amazed her. Was she really so lost to reason? Apparently, the answer was yes.

When he entered her, reality narrowed to Vaughn's face—his fierce, brilliant green eyes—the flash of white teeth when he smiled. The labored sound of his breathing.

In that moment when their bodies joined completely, flesh to flesh, heart to heart, there was a hush in the room. Almost as if everything that had been out of kilter in Brie's world finally settled into place. Such thinking was self-defeating, but she couldn't shake the notion that this man was her soul mate.

How pathetic was that?

Thinking and reasoning were a lost cause, anyway. All she wanted to do right now was *feel*. And heaven help her, there were *so* many feelings. His skin was hot against hers, his breath warm on her cheek. When he buried his face in the curve of her neck and groaned, the sound reverberated throughout her body.

She loved making him lose control, always had. In the past, they had made love often two and three times a day. She'd had no way of knowing precisely when he actually made her pregnant. She used to imagine which time it had been. Where they were. How it had felt.

The result of their passion lay sleeping just down the hall. Brie and Vaughn had created that—how perfect, how wonderful, how unbearably poignant.

She dragged her attention back to the present, more than content to live in the moment, at least for now. A lock of Vaughn's hair had fallen across his damp forehead. She pushed it back, so close to him she could see the tiny flecks of amber in his deep-emerald irises.

"I've missed being with you," she whispered. Maybe later she would regret her honesty, but it was true.

He kissed her again, bruising her lips, thrusting his tongue against hers in desperation, the same desperation she felt. "God, yes."

He felt huge and hard inside her. Intimidating. In charge. But she wanted this. More than anything. She wasn't afraid of Vaughn Blackwood. Not at all.

Nothing he had ever said or done to her had made her fear his physical domination. Despite his size and the fact that he outweighed her significantly, his care with her during their lovemaking—past and present—made her feel safe and cherished even in the midst of their wildest passion.

Then, in a flash, it was over. They were both too close to the edge, both too needy to make it last.

Vaughn cursed ruefully. "Sorry," he muttered. "Were you…did I…" His uncustomary awkwardness surprised her.

"I'm good." And physically, she was. Emotionally?

The weirdness was back. Two years apart. A baby. A man who wanted to be free.

Tears stung her eyes.

Vaughn nuzzled his face between her breasts. "It's not enough," he said hoarsely. "I want more."

"We don't have any more condoms."

She saw on his face that he had forgotten. "There are other ways," he whispered, licking her nipple until it budded hard and tight. "Why don't I go clean up and then we'll improvise?"

When he separated their bodies, Brie felt the disconnect as a physical pain. "Okay." She should have said an emphatic no. Any smart woman would have. But Brie was caught up in an erotic web of longing and need. "I'll wait for you."

Eight

Vaughn staggered into Brie's tiny hallway bathroom, hoping she hadn't noticed that his legs were rubbery. He felt drunk. Out of control. Completely off his game.

Was he insane to stay the night and keep fooling around? They had no more protection. None. He couldn't slide inside her warm, tight body and empty himself in spasms of intense pleasure.

He was no teenage kid willing to come any way he could manage. A grown man had needs.

But if the alternative to full sexual contact with his lover was to walk out of this house right now, he couldn't do it. Not when Brie had finally burst back into his life.

Vaughn dealt with the condom and washed up, finishing by splashing water in his face. When he looked in the mirror, his eyes glittered with strong emotion.

Was it exhilaration he saw? Simple lust? How could a man not understand his own responses?

He needed Brie. He wanted her. Nothing beyond tonight mattered. He would deal with the future later.

When he returned to the bedroom, he found Brie huddled up against the headboard with the sheet pulled to her chin. Her eyes widened as her gaze dropped to his erection. Was it excitement or fear he saw in her baby blue irises?

He joined her on the bed. "I won't do anything you don't like, Brie."

"That's what I'm afraid of." Her wry smile touched him.

The note of humor defused some of the tension in the room but did nothing to reduce his hunger for her. Slowly, he dragged the sheet away. Even though he'd already memorized the feel of her body against his, there was nothing he could do to muffle his sharp inhalation at the view. The sight of her was a punch to the gut. He wrapped two hands around her ankle and slowly pulled her down in the bed.

"Turn over," he said softly.

After a moment's hesitation, she did as he asked, her arms stretched over her head.

Now he didn't have to disguise his reactions and his intent. Lord, she was beautiful. Her body was lithe and strong, her waist narrow above flared hips that had cradled their baby.

He put two hands on her ass and massaged her heart-shaped backside. Brie made a tiny noise, but she didn't try to stop him. Her skin was soft and smooth.

Though he wanted to pounce and gobble her up, he focused on giving her pleasure. Moving his hands slowly, he kneaded her tense muscles from waist to shoulders, coaxing her body into limp surrender. She worked hard. For tonight, he wanted to make her forget everything but how good it felt to be naked in bed with a lover. With him.

The more Brie responded to his massage, the harder he got. *She* might be relaxed, but this exercise was having the opposite effect on Vaughn. He changed positions and started on her thighs and calves.

His breathing roughened. His hands shook. When he couldn't bear it a second more, he rolled her onto her back and kissed her with long, slow, drugging kisses.

He came perilously close to sliding inside her without protection. His arousal was a living, breathing ache. Doggedly, he clamped down on his carnal impulses. He'd promised they could improvise. He was a man of his word.

When he parted her legs and kissed the inside of her thigh, Brie squeaked in shock. "Relax, sweetheart. You'll ruin the effects of the massage."

Her fingers clenched in the sheet. "How can I relax with you doing that?"

They had often enjoyed this game in the past. While the act embarrassed her initially, experience said that she'd warm up to it quickly. He knew exactly how to give her what she wanted. In minutes, she was crying out his name and arching into his caress.

With her shoulders pressed to the mattress and her

hips lifting to his touch, she came beautifully. He could have watched her forever…held her forever.

He cuddled her against his body, warming her chilled limbs. "Good?" he asked, though the question was perhaps self-serving.

She nodded sleepily, nuzzling his hair-roughened chest. "Oh yeah. As soon as I can breathe again, I'll return the favor."

He could have said no. She was a single mom with a small child and a full-time job. Brie needed her sleep.

But apparently Vaughn was a selfish bastard, even now. When Brie knelt over him with her silky hair brushing his shoulders, he groaned aloud. In some ways, what they were about to do was more intimate and arousing than before.

When she slid down his body and began circling the head of his shaft with her teeth and nibbling gently, his scalp tightened. Everything else in his body from the cell level on up tensed in helpless anticipation.

Brie was inventive and determined to torture him. Every time he was on the verge of exploding, she drew back…slowed the pace.

He cursed and begged.

Her low laugh made the hair on his body stand up, his skin tingling. This was why they had practically screwed themselves to death during their wild and wanton association when she worked at the ranch. Their relationship may have failed, but when it came to *this*, they were incendiary together. Perfectly matched.

At last, when he was incoherent with lust, she leaned

back on her heels, took him in a firm grip and finished him off. His climax was painfully intense.

He groaned her name.

When he came to his senses, Brie was at his side, curled into him, one leg sprawled across his thighs. She stroked his chest. "You have to go home," she said. There was no inflection in the words.

"I know." He wanted to argue. Wanted to stay right where he was. But he was a pragmatist. No matter how much the truth sucked, it was still the truth.

When he thought his legs would support him, he rolled out of bed, gathered his shirt and pants and the rest, and made a second trip to the bathroom. This time when he returned, Brie was *not* in the bed. She had donned a silky nightgown and a fleecy robe and was standing by the dresser brushing her hair.

Nothing about her stance was deliberately provocative. Didn't matter. He wanted her still. With as much desperation as he had an hour before. Being with her tonight hadn't appeased his hunger. It had only reminded him of everything he was missing.

She stared at him from across the room, her expression sober. "I can't have an affair with you, Vaughn. Even if I wanted to, it would be impossible. You see that, right?"

"I suppose." He felt sulky and out of sorts. Which was a damned shame considering his recent euphoria. "But there's more at stake here than our physical relationship."

"What do you mean?"

"In my father's will, there was a letter to me. And

something he said… I don't quite understand it, but I got the sense there may be twists and turns when it comes to Dad's inheritance. Like maybe we were all on probation. Kellan is happily married now. Sophie will tie the knot soon. If I'm the only one left, I think you and I should get engaged. Not really," he said quickly. "Only for show. So Miranda can see that I'm as stable and settled as the rest of them."

"Why? You said you don't care about the money."

"I don't, for myself. But when Dad died, he had no idea Danika existed. My daughter—*our* daughter," he said, "is entitled to my share of the money. I want her to have it."

"You and I both have good jobs. We don't need Buckley's money."

"I agree. We don't. But that inheritance will secure Danika's future. It doesn't make sense to let it slip through our fingers."

"If you trot out a fake engagement, everyone in town will be talking about us. It's not the kind of thing Royal will keep quiet."

"True. But you and I can stand a bit of gossip. For our daughter's sake." His throat tightened with unexpected emotion. "I've missed almost two years of her life, Brie. I want to do this for my child, my own flesh and blood. You can understand that."

Brie didn't seem convinced, but he wouldn't back down on this point. She nodded slowly. "If you're sure."

"As soon as the inheritance is settled, I'll set up a trust fund for Nika. Then we can break off the engagement, and I'll head back to Fort Worth. End of story."

Brie stared at him, her head cocked to one side. "Aren't you afraid people in Royal will expect you to marry me? That's why we broke up before. You wanted absolutely no ties or responsibility."

His heart skipped a couple of beats and settled into a sluggish rhythm. Sweat dampened his forehead. "That wouldn't happen. You wouldn't use the court of public opinion."

"Never underestimate an enemy. You taught me that, Vaughn. It's high on your list of business maxims." Perhaps sensing his unease, she chuckled softly. "Don't worry, big guy. I'd never force anyone to marry me. When I get engaged for real, I want a man who is one hundred percent invested in our relationship. That's not too much to ask."

He studied her for a long time as the silence between them grew. It wasn't too much to ask. Not at all. But Vaughn wasn't that guy. Still, when he tried to imagine Brie, blonde and beautiful in a wedding dress, walking down the aisle to meet the man of her dreams, his stomach curled in dread.

Maybe this engagement wasn't a good idea after all. It would put the two of them in the midst of a fake intimacy that might coax him into doing something dangerous.

But no, he couldn't back down out of base fear. He had to do this—for his daughter's sake. He cleared his throat. "So you agree? To the engagement, I mean."

She nodded slowly. "I agree. But what about Sophie's wedding? And the flower girl thing?"

"I think we go ahead with it. It will cement our..." He trailed off, unwilling to say the word.

Brie had no such scruples. "Cement our lie. That's what you wanted to say, right?"

Why did she keep pushing him? "My sister wants Nika in the wedding, so that's what we'll do. I'll tell Sophie we're engaged."

"And what about Kellan? If Sophie knows, you wouldn't keep him in the dark, would you?"

"No. I'll swing by there in the morning and fill him in."

"And Dixie?"

Damn. This was getting complicated already. "Her, too."

The fact that he didn't have a longer list of family and friends in which to confide underscored Dixie's description of his personality. He couldn't decide if that was a bad thing or a good thing.

Brie yawned. The smudges beneath her eyes did nothing to detract from her wholesome beauty, but they told him she was exhausted. Time for a graceful exit.

He wanted to kiss her again. Badly. He was on the way out the door, so surely indulging his impulse wouldn't lead him astray.

Crossing the room in two strides, he removed the hairbrush from her hand and set it aside. When she seemed startled, he grimaced. "A good-night kiss. That's all."

As he pulled her against his chest, Brie sighed and groaned. That sound encompassed every bit of frustration and resignation he felt at the thought of stepping away from her and walking out that door. Even clothed, her body was an almost irresistible temptation.

Her arms wound around his neck. Her hair, silky and thick, tumbled down her back. He tangled his hands in the strands, gripping convulsively as if he could make the moment last.

She tilted back her head, and their lips met, almost tentatively at first. This chaste farewell was something beyond his experience. He was filled with awe and tenderness. Passion was there, simmering beneath the surface. But for long seconds, he offered her his...*affection*, not his male hunger.

This woman had given him a daughter. A child who might well be the only legacy he had to leave behind one day.

"Brie..." he muttered her name, not at all sure he had anything to say that would please her, but infinitely certain he didn't want to hurt her with his silence.

She stroked the back of his neck, sending chills throughout his body. "It's okay, Vaughn. You can't be something you're not. Neither can I. You'll be leaving soon. I'm happy we're not at odds anymore."

Her speech unsettled him in ways he didn't understand. But more importantly, the way her body clung to his gave him a rush of exultation. In spite of everything that had gone wrong between them, her body still wanted his.

He pulled her more tightly against him. In her bare feet, she was small. Vulnerable. But when he looked into her eyes, he realized he was at risk, as well.

"Kiss me again," he begged. "One for the road."

"You're not going off to war," she teased.

He moved his mouth over hers softly. "If I go head-to-head with the stepwitch, it might as well be mortal combat."

She cupped his face in her hands and petted him, her fingertips exploring the late-night stubble she found on his chin. "Hating Miranda has become a habit for you, Vaughn. She's not evil. I doubt if she's even avaricious."

"Maybe. Can we quit mentioning my former step-mother?"

"You brought her up, not me."

Vaughn nipped Brie's bottom lip, then stroked the tiny sting with his tongue. "I don't want to go," he said roughly, undone by the hour and the woman and the many months they had spent apart.

Brie broke free of the embrace and stepped back, putting physical distance between them to mirror the emotional distance he had always insisted upon. Light. Casual. Nothing to tie a man down.

Suddenly, Vaughn flashed to a vision of his father, wasting away in his bed. The old man's once-sturdy frame frail and helpless. Alone at the end. Vaughn shuddered, more shaken than he cared to admit by the grim image.

You're probably the most like me. Buckley's words echoed in Vaughn's head, haunting him from beyond the grave. Vaughn hadn't actually *witnessed* his father on his deathbed. A housekeeper had discovered the body and called the coroner.

Buckley Blackwood had been ensconced in a pricey casket at the funeral home when his children saw him next. The patriarch, dressed in a tailored suit, had looked imposing even in that situation.

Vaughn swallowed hard and shook off the feeling that a ghost had crossed his path. Buckley wouldn't be here tonight trying to influence the outcome. Two years ago, Buck had hated the idea of his son having *any* kind of a relationship with Brielle. He'd believed the Blackwood clan was Texas royalty. Better than most folks. Certainly far above Brielle's station in life.

The woman in question frowned slightly, looking concerned. "Are you okay, Vaughn? You zoned out on me there for a minute."

He cleared his throat. "I'm fine," he said gruffly.

"I don't suppose we'll see each other much between now and the wedding rehearsal," she said.

"I'll be around."

Her lips twitched in a reluctant smile. "Threat? Or promise?"

He walked toward the door. "You'll just have to find out."

Nine

Sophie poured milk into her Cheerios and stirred them glumly. "Tell me again why we didn't just elope?"

Nigel dropped a kiss on top of his fiancée's head and joined her at the small table in the breakfast nook. His plate of perfectly browned toast with butter and marmalade was arranged neatly. "Because you, my love, wanted a big wedding with all the frills."

"Why didn't you stop me?" she wailed. "What was I thinking?"

Unfortunately, Nigel had heard this lament before. "It's going to be brilliant, darling girl. You're just getting cold feet. I'm told it's a common problem for brides."

"I *want* to marry you," she insisted. "But why do we need the big ceremony? You've never been to Vegas. We could be there before nightfall."

Nigel gave her a British version of the stink eye. "Eat your breakfast." He turned up his nose at her choice. "If you can call it that."

"Cheerios are healthy," she said indignantly.

"Not when you dump six teaspoons of sugar into the bowl." His shudder was theatrical.

The Englishman had her there. She'd always had a sweet tooth. Not that he seemed to mind her fuller curves—especially when they were in bed together. Her cheeks heated as memories of last night flashed through her brain.

Nigel's smirking grin told her he knew exactly what she was thinking. The man had an annoying habit of reading her mind.

"I need a break," she said. "From all the wedding nonsense. Vaughn wants to take Brie to Dallas overnight. I sort of promised to keep the baby while they're gone."

Nigel blinked, his smile fading. "As in babysit?"

"Yes. We're both intelligent adults. Surely we can muddle through. It will be fun."

"She's not even two, is she? I wouldn't have the slightest notion of what to do with her. Besides, my family will be here soon. We've lots to do in the meantime."

"Don't you see? That's why I'm freaking out. We'll be showing everyone around, wining and dining them. And after that, it will be time for the wedding rehearsal. I need to take my mind off the madness. I want to play house with you. Who knows, maybe we'll decide we want a little one of our own."

He paled. "Good lord, Sophie. Are you trying to

tell me you're…?" He swallowed hard and dropped his toast.

"Pregnant?" She laughed softly. "No, silly man. But I don't want to wait long, do you?"

He stood abruptly, scooped her out of her chair and carried her toward the bedroom.

Sophie pretended to be outraged. "Put me down. My cereal will get soggy."

Nigel tossed her onto the bed and started ripping off his clothes. "You said you didn't want to wait too long. I'm here to fulfill your every whim."

Sophie's heart overflowed with happiness. How had she gotten so damn lucky? She blinked back tears. "I love you, Nigel Townshend. Till death do us part."

His smile was tight and feral. "And I you, my crazy, gorgeous American bride. Now quit talking so I can ravish you."

Brie felt as if she was balanced on the edge of a precipice. The view was incredible, but she was terrified of falling.

Vaughn was true to his word. He'd made getting to know his daughter a priority. But he also had insisted on bringing dinner in most evenings, so Brie wouldn't have to worry about cooking after a long day at the veterinarian office.

Not only that, but the meals hadn't been pizza and burgers, which were her usual go-tos when she needed a break. He'd tracked down a private chef who catered to families with organic farm-to-table foods that kids would eat.

His thoughtfulness touched Brie.

Even so, she was cautious around him. Their breakup before Nika was born had traumatized her. She'd felt adrift. Completely lost. No matter how much she tried to convince herself otherwise, those strong feelings for Vaughn still simmered below the surface.

She was older now, though. Stronger. She had a responsibility to Danika that had to come before anything and everyone else.

Oddly enough, Vaughn didn't press the physical issue. He was affectionate and amusing and an all-around entertaining guest time and again. It wasn't his fault that Brie spent hours each night tossing and turning because she missed him in her bed.

What was he waiting for?

Maybe, like Brie, he was feeling cautious, because their behavior affected more than just themselves.

Brie and Vaughn *had* argued over the issue of childcare. Vaughn insisted that as his daughter, Danika should attend the state-of-the-art day care center at the Texas Cattleman's Club. Brie thought such an arrangement was too public a declaration of something she wasn't entirely ready for the world to know.

The thing that convinced her in the end was not Vaughn's persistence, but rather the fact that Brie knew it was time for Nika to begin playing with other children. The almost two-year-old was smart and happy and well-adjusted, but she needed more opportunities for socialization. The Club's childcare was second to none.

In the end, Brie agreed that Vaughn could pick up Nika two mornings a week and drop her off at the club.

Since he had bought an expensive car seat for his vehicle, there wasn't much else Brie could find to protest.

The babysitter had actually been relieved to cut back on her hours. She was an older woman, and Nika's nonstop energy could be tiring to deal with.

So now, Brie's days were running even more smoothly.

The big change today was that Vaughn had unexpectedly asked to meet her for lunch. Thursdays were her half days at the clinic. Brie closed up shop at twelve thirty sharp, knowing that Dr. Brody would reopen the office at two. She slipped out of her lab coat and into a black blazer that matched her pants.

Tomorrow and every other Friday, Doc Brody covered for her. That usually gave Brie a chance to spend more time with Danika and to catch up on life in general.

Vaughn was in the reception area leafing through a magazine when she found him. "Hey," she said, wincing inwardly at the breathless tone in her voice.

He stood slowly and looked at her with that masculine smile that melted her knees. "Hey, yourself. Are you hungry?"

"Actually, starving." She flipped her hair from underneath her collar. "We had more appointments than usual, probably because it's right before the weekend. People don't want to wait any longer if they're worried something is wrong."

He took her arm as they exited the building. "You love what you do, don't you? Even though you used to work with big animals at Blackwood Hollow?"

She nodded. "I do. Horses were always my favorite,

but a general veterinarian practice is more practical for a mom with young children. Normal hours make a huge difference. And besides, this work is rewarding, too. Pet owners are wonderful people. It gives me a lot of personal satisfaction to make someone's cat or dog well again. Or even the occasional ferret."

Vaughn fell back a step and stared at her. "Seriously?"

Brie laughed. "Of course. I've dealt with boa constrictors, parrots…you name it."

He took her arm again and steered her toward the restaurant where they had reservations. It was a quiet, out-of-the way French bistro. Definitely a special-occasion kind of restaurant. Not the kind of spot where construction workers dropped by on their lunch breaks.

Brie had never actually eaten here. When she walked inside and saw the upscale decor and elegant furnishings, her internal radar went off. Why was Vaughn taking her to lunch at such an unabashedly romantic venue?

He held her chair for her, his hand brushing her shoulder as she was seated. The fleeting touch sent shivers down her spine.

She picked up her menu and studied it intently, unable to meet his gaze. He watched her with a small smile that made her toes curl. Finally, she'd had enough. "What?" she demanded quietly, conscious of other diners nearby.

Vaughn lifted one shoulder in an elegant shrug. He was wearing a dark suit with a yellow tie and a pristine white shirt—hopefully not the one Danika had ruined.

"I like looking at you," he said. "When we're with

our daughter, we tend to make her the focus of our attention, as it should be. And we're always careful not to wake her. But I thought it would be nice to have a few minutes alone together away from the house."

She chewed her lip, not trusting his casual amiability. The old Vaughn would never have wanted time alone in the midst of other people. He would have found a much more private spot for the two of them to get naked and slake their mutual need.

"I appreciate the invitation," she said, her tone carefully noncommittal. "I only had a banana for breakfast."

Immediately, Vaughn summoned their waiter. "The lady would like to order, please."

Over the salad course, Brielle could contain her curiosity no longer. She lowered her voice and leaned toward him. "You might as well tell me what's going on. I know you, Vaughn Blackwood. You've got something up your sleeve."

He buttered a piece of crusty bread and handed it to her. "I have a request, I'll admit. I thought you'd be more open to my proposal if you weren't hungry."

"Am I so predictable?" Though she was loath to admit it, Vaughn knew *her*, too. Which made it hard to hide her feelings and reactions from him.

"Don't be grumpy, Brie. I have a surprise for you. If you're willing."

Her knees pressed together under the table, and her palms got sweaty. "I don't like surprises."

"I remember," he said ruefully. "Canceling those tickets to the Fiji Islands at the last minute cost me a bundle."

"You should have known better. There was no way I was going to simply run off to Vanua Levu with you for two weeks."

"Too many rules, woman. Living a spontaneous life is more fun."

"Sorry. The idea never held much appeal for me. Which is just as well, since it's not an option anymore. Any shot I had at living a spontaneous life ended when Danika was born…at least for several years in the future. Small children thrive on familiar routines and boring schedules. You're free, Vaughn. I'm not."

He drained his wineglass and raised his hand for more. The quick frown that shadowed his face when she talked about not being free vanished quickly, but Brie had witnessed his discomfort with the topic.

Before the discussion could resume, a waiter returned with their perfectly cooked filet mignon and twice-baked potatoes. The food was stunningly good.

Brie dug in, happy to have a respite from the awkward conversation. "Danika is loving the childcare center at the club," she said. "Thanks for suggesting it."

Vaughn chewed and swallowed, then took a sip of wine. Brie knew she was in trouble when she fixated on the ripple of muscles in his tanned throat. She had a terrible urge to nibble his neck all the way to his beautiful mouth. And stay there.

Forcing herself to look away, she concentrated instead on finishing her meal. It was easier to eat than talk. No land mines in culinary excess. Silence was golden.

Her dining partner responded at last. "You're welcome. I thought she would like the center. Kellan and Sophie and I have several friends who have already started families. For the couples where both parents work outside the home, it's very comforting to know your child is in good hands. Or so I'm told."

Brielle couldn't wait any longer. Who knew how soon dessert would arrive? "Tell me," she said, sitting back in her chair and dabbing her lips with a snowy-white linen napkin. "What's the surprise?"

Vaughn reached across the table and took her hand. Brie was so startled she didn't even take it back. His grasp was warm and firm. Perhaps she should pull free, but it was so much nicer to let the man take charge just this once.

"I want you to go to Dallas with me. Overnight." His green eyes gleamed.

That last word was fraught with meaning. "Why?"

He grinned. "For fun. Or more accurately, for work and play. I have two meetings I need to be there for. One will include you. You'll need to bring fancy clothes. Or I can take you shopping."

That sounded delightful, but Vaughn's pricey gifts always came with strings. "I have plenty of clothes," she said wryly. "But it's a moot point. I can't leave town on a whim. I have a daughter and a medical practice."

"I've got it all under control," he said. "Tomorrow is Dr. Brody's day to cover for you, remember? Even better, Sophie and Nigel have volunteered to keep Nika overnight. Sophie is thrilled."

"But what about all the wedding festivities? Nigel's whole family is arriving from England Sunday evening.

We can't ask them to babysit when they have so much going on. It's too much."

"It was my idea, but Sophie's jumped on it. She's sick to death of all the wedding details. She swears that focusing on keeping Danika for thirty-six hours will give her a much-needed break. We'll be back to put our daughter to bed Saturday night. Sophie and Nigel will have time to catch their breath before all the revelry continues."

"I can't imagine Nigel Townshend changing Nika's *nappies*, as they say."

"You misjudge my future brother-in-law. I've watched them together. That poor bloke will do absolutely anything for my sister. He's head-over-ass *smitten* with her."

"I can't decide if that makes you happy or if you think less of him for his devotion."

"Of course I'm happy. She's my sister."

"But you would never be all gaga over a woman, would you, Vaughn?"

His gaze narrowed. "Are you trying to pick a fight with me, Brielle?"

She stared at him, torn in half a dozen directions. Trusting Sophie with Danika wasn't a huge obstacle. Vaughn's sister had a natural affinity for children. She used to babysit all the time as a teenager.

Even being away from Royal and the vet clinic wasn't a problem. Vaughn was right. Brie had already planned to be off tomorrow. So why was she hesitating?

It all boiled down to one simple fact.

"You mean for this trip to include sex, right?"

He blinked, and his neck turned red. "I hadn't planned on announcing it to the whole restaurant, but yes. Is that a deal breaker?"

He was ruffled. Brie liked that. A lot. "Yes, I'll go," she said. "And yes, we'll have sex. Spontaneous trysts are romantic. Count me in."

Ten

Miranda Dupree was desperately glad to be back in the Big Apple. She loved Royal. Always had. But now that half the town thought she was a scheming hussy, it wasn't much fun anymore.

The three official Blackwood offspring were angry in varying degrees. As for Darius, the illegitimate son—he and Miranda had a good working relationship, necessary for the planned partnership between their businesses. But as he'd told her, he sided with his half siblings in his frustration over the whole tangle with Buck's will. From an adult child's perspective, she supposed it made sense. Their father had created an impossible situation and dragged Miranda into the middle of a mess, whether she liked it or not.

Worst of all, Buck's convoluted plan meant that everyone viewed her as a villain without knowing the truth of what Buck wanted her to do with her inheritance. Sometimes, she wondered why she was putting up with it all. The fact that Buckley had made a huge bequest to her charity, Girl to the Nth Power, was the only thing that made the past few months at all palatable.

It was noon, and Miranda had already stopped in at the Girl Power offices. Things always got a little sloppy when she was out of town. Probably because she was a micromanager. She had tried to do better in that regard, thanks to urging from her therapist.

Girl to the Nth Power and Goddess Inc., her burgeoning health and lifestyle brand, were her babies. When she walked away from her marriage to Buckley Blackwood, she'd wanted to make her own way in the world. An airtight prenup gave her little choice.

Fortunately, wise investments on her part when she was still *Mrs.* Blackwood meant she had a safety net. She was proud of the life she had built in New York. But her therapist was right. The pace she kept these days was in danger of ruining her health and her happiness.

Both organizations needed capable, trustworthy CEOs at the helm full-time. Miranda needed and wanted to step back. It had been so long since she'd had a day off, she'd forgotten what it was like to go to the Hamptons for the weekend. Or simply to hole up in her three-thousand-square-foot apartment near Seventy-Sixth and Madison and do nothing but enjoy a bubble bath and a good book.

Unfortunately, that day off wasn't coming any time

soon. Until she discharged her responsibilities as Buckley's heir, she had *more* work to do, not less.

Things were chugging right along at Goddess Inc., though the staff seemed startled to see her. Not a bad thing. Miranda believed in running a tight ship. She was strict but fair.

Unfortunately, the daily business of health and lifestyle centers seemed to be doing fine without her. Which meant she had to face the truth. The only reason she was still puttering around in her office with the view of Central Park was that she was afraid to face Kai Maddox.

"Kai." She whispered the syllable out loud, trying to reduce its power.

Once upon a time, before she was married to Buck, Kai had been her whole world. With his scarred jaw from an old motorcycle accident and neatly inked tattoos covering his muscular biceps, he was the epitome of the bad boy who drew women like bees to honey.

Dark brown hair. Brown eyes. His olive complexion, courtesy of his Mexican roots, added to his moody charm. Though a scowl was his habitual expression, when he smiled… *Oh, lordy.* The man was gorgeous.

He was also a skilled hacker. Though he had come perilously close at one time to ending up on the wrong side of the law, he was now a widely respected cybersecurity expert.

Miranda was worried about Blackwood Bank. Since inheriting the business from Buck, she'd looked into the paperwork and noticed a few irregularities recently. Enough to make her realize that she needed Kai's help.

Her covert snooping had established that Kai was actually in New York this week, speaking to a high-profile meeting of police officers and detectives from all over the country about the kind of tech stuff that made Miranda's head hurt.

Her plan was to show up unannounced at Kai's hotel later tonight and ask for his help. She was hoping that enough time had passed for him to forget the fact that she had gone from his bed to Buckley's.

In her defense, Kai had checked out on the relationship months before Miranda let herself be enticed by Buckley's determined courtship. But the end result was still the same—she'd married Buck and left behind the life she'd known before. If Kai was holding on to any resentment over that, working with him would be… challenging.

To say Kai had issues was an understatement. The chip on his shoulder was large enough to start a hundred fires. Build a dozen ships. Maybe if Miranda had met him at a different time in his life…

The next hours passed with agonizing slowness. Even Madison Avenue shopping, one of her go-to stress relievers, didn't do the trick. She bought a new outfit just for the heck of it, ignoring the huge wardrobe that filled a closet and a half in her apartment.

This meeting with Kai was important. The fire-engine red strapless dress fit her almost too well. Her ample breasts were in danger of spilling out. When she added black patent leather stilettos with tiny rhinestones on the heels, she couldn't decide if the image she presented was bodacious bombshell or tacky tramp.

Either way, Kai was in for a shock.

In the cab heading across town, she found herself wishing she had downed a good stiff drink to give her courage.

It had been years since she and Kai had been face-to-face with each other. Would she be able to convince him to help her?

Thankfully, she had the advantage of surprise. Kai wasn't the only one with street smarts. Miranda still knew guys from the old days. One of them, ironically named Digger, was a huge Yankees fan. Miranda had bought a couple of behind–home plate tickets yesterday for the season opener and offered them to Digger. All he had to do was hack into the hotel's database and find a room number.

Digger loved it. He thought he was facilitating a lovers' tryst. Or at least a booty call. Miranda didn't care what Digger thought.

In the mirrored elevator, she checked her hair and makeup. With her fiery tresses, the dress probably clashed, but she had never let that bother her. The more wince-worthy realization was the way her cleavage looked, well…deep.

Kai had always been a boob man, by his own admission. Perhaps subconsciously Miranda had picked this dress for just that reason.

Her legs were wobbly when she stood in front of room 8902. It was a suite. Of course. The man had come up in the world. Way up.

She took a deep, decidedly unsteady breath and knocked. Kai answered immediately. His hair was ruffled as if he had been sprawled on the sofa watching TV to relax. That sounded like him.

But any relaxation faded when he saw her. His eyes flashed, and the permanent furrow in his brow deepened. "Oh, hell no," he said.

When he tried to close the door in her face, she stuck a leg through the opening, risking amputation. "I need to speak with you," she said. "About business."

Perhaps the fact that her voice went all low and husky made her claim slightly unbelievable.

He shook his head in disbelief. "Only you, Miranda. I can't believe you had the balls to come here after everything that has happened. Am I finally gonna get an apology from you?"

Her blood pressure shot to the stratosphere. "Me? Apologize? For what? For walking away from a relationship you'd already killed? You were the distant, angry one." She stopped short and took a deep breath. "I'm here with legitimate business. Will you talk to me? Civilly?"

A spark flamed hot in those rich chocolate pupils. "I don't do business with cheaters," he said roughly. "There's only one thing women like you are good for."

"So you do remember that part?" she taunted. She ran a fingertip along his bottom lip, helpless to resist the feelings his nearness evoked.

"You'd better leave right now," he said, his gaze wild with strong emotion.

"Or what?"

He dragged her close against his body, tilted back

her head and slammed his lips down on hers. As kisses went, it was world-class. Volcanoes erupted. Flash fires ignited. The earth's orbit accelerated.

Miranda never would have believed such heat could remain between them after so many years. She went soft and limp in his embrace. Kai was anything *but* soft. She might have whimpered embarrassingly when he cupped a breast in one big palm and squeezed.

Ten seconds passed. Maybe thirty. Time became fluid. He tasted exactly the same. And for a brief, insane moment in time, she became the young, naive girl she had been when they first met.

He could have dragged her into the room and onto the bed and she might not have stopped him.

But he didn't.

Kai broke the kiss abruptly and wiped his mouth. His face lost all expression, though muscles rippled in his throat, and his chest heaved. "The answer is no, Miranda. Not me. Not you. Business be damned. I wouldn't cross the street for you. Not anymore."

Then he set her gently into the hall, closed the door and turned the dead bolt. The loud *snick* snapped her out of a trance.

Humiliation and regret washed through her like the flu, churning her stomach and giving her a headache. There was nothing to do but retreat. She would have to find another way to protect Blackwood Bank. But how?

Kai had been her only real hope for someone she could trust to investigate without causing gossip about the bank.

Her spine stiffened, and she wiped her eyes, careful not to smear her mascara. He hadn't heard the last of her. She hadn't gotten where she was in the world by letting herself get pushed around. He *would* help her. Eventually.

Because she wasn't going to give up on him. Not this time.

Brie strapped herself into the seat beside Vaughn and wondered if all mothers felt the same when going on a trip with their partner and leaving their child behind. Torn between love for their babies and the men they cared about. Husbands. Lovers. Fathers.

She had never left Nika overnight before. When she and Vaughn dropped Danika off at Sophie's house and swapped the car seat, Brie nearly cried. She felt guilty, because she was excited to be going to Dallas with Vaughn.

Nika, on the other hand, had barely said goodbye to her mother. She was already playing with the pile of toys Sophie had somehow procured in an incredibly short time.

Now, Brie was sitting in the front of a terrifyingly small plane while her daughter's father went calmly through a preflight checklist. "I had no idea we weren't flying commercial," she said.

His cocky sideways grin amused her. "I might have omitted that info, because I wasn't sure you would come if you knew. But I promise, you can trust me. I've logged hundreds of hours of flight time. And besides, once we're airborne, you'll see how wonderful it is to chase the clouds."

He sounded almost poetic. If she hadn't been anxious and uncertain about her decision to join him, she might have appreciated his promises more. As it was, her hands were clenched on the armrests and her teeth had chewed a raw place on her bottom lip.

Though takeoff left her stomach on the ground, Vaughn was right. In this small plane, it felt as if the two of them were dancing across the sky. They didn't talk to each other, but the silence felt comfortable and natural. It was enough to watch Vaughn's big, masculine hands on the controls and to take in the view outside.

The flight was uneventful until they were thirty minutes outside Dallas. Suddenly, Vaughn cursed, his jaw tight.

"What's wrong?" Brie cried.

"I'm not sure," he said, flipping dials and switches. "The fuel indicator has gone all wonky, and my oil pressure is dropping. We may have to make an emergency landing."

The way he said those words was exactly the tone of voice a man would use to say *I may have to pull off the road and get some gas.*

Brie's brain spun wildly, trying to process the words. Even she could tell that their airspeed was dropping. "Can we make it to the airport?"

"Doubtful." He picked up the radio and called the tower. A flash of incomprehensible conversation left her more worried, not less. When the radio went silent,

Vaughn reached out and squeezed her hand. "I've done this in a simulator."

Her eyes rounded. "Done what?"

"Put a plane down in a field. If my calculations are right, we'll be just short of the runway. But the surrounding acreage is flat. We should be fine."

Every disaster movie she had ever seen flashed through her brain. The fire engines and rescue squad vehicles tearing down the runways, sirens blaring. The escape slide being deployed. But this tin can they were in barely even had a door, much less an escape plan—or at least, one she could visualize.

Brie's prayer life took a real turn. "Tell me Nika is not going to be an orphan," she begged.

"Not if I can help it." The words were terse. This time he didn't look at her. He was too busy for that.

The next ten minutes unfolded with both agonizing slowness and terrifying speed. He reached in a cabinet beside him and pulled out a folded blanket. "Put your face in this. All the way down to your knees. Hands over your head."

When she hesitated, he shouted at her, "Now."

The ground rushed up at them. There was nothing in sight but a stubbly cornfield.

Vaughn cursed and shouted a Mayday call into the radio.

Then they crashed. Hard.

Intellectually, she understood that Vaughn had deployed the landing gear. But without a smooth runway, it felt as if they were catapulting nose over tail.

The world spun dizzily, filled with the noise of

"One Minute" Survey

GET YOUR FREE BOOKS AND FREE GIFTS!

✓ Complete this Survey ✓ Return this survey

▼ DETACH AND MAIL CARD TODAY! ▼

1 Do you try to find time to read every day?

☐ YES ☐ NO

2 Do you prefer stories with happy endings?

☐ YES ☐ NO

3 Do you enjoy having books delivered to your home?

☐ YES ☐ NO

4 Do you share your favorite books with friends?

☐ YES ☐ NO

YES! I have completed the above "One Minute" Survey. Please send me my Two Free Books and Two Free Mystery Gifts (worth over $20 retail). I understand that I am under no obligation to buy anything, as explained on the back of this card.

225/326 HDL GNNS

FIRST NAME LAST NAME

ADDRESS

APT.# CITY

STATE/PROV. ZIP/POSTAL CODE

Offer limited to one per household and not applicable to series that subscriber is currently receiving. **Your Privacy**—The Reader Service is committed to protecting your privacy. Our Privacy Policy is available online at www.ReaderService.com or upon request from the Reader Service. We make a portion of our mailing list available to reputable third parties that offer products we believe may interest you. If you prefer that we not exchange your name with third parties, or if you wish to clarify or modify your communication preferences, please visit us at www.ReaderService.com/consumerschoice or write to us at Reader Service Preference Service, P.O. Box 9062, Buffalo, NY 14240-9062. Include your complete name and address.

HD-220-OM20

READER SERVICE—**Here's how it works:**

Accepting your 2 free Harlequin Desire® books and 2 free gifts (gifts valued at approximately $10.00 retail) places you under no obligation to buy anything. You may keep the books and gifts and return the shipping statement marked "cancel." If you do not cancel, about a month later we'll send you 6 additional books and bill you just $4.55 each in the U.S. or $5.24 each in Canada. That is a savings of at least 13% off the cover price. It's quite a bargain! Shipping and handling is just 50¢ per book in the U.S. and $1.25 per book in Canada*. You may cancel at any time, but if you choose to continue, every month we'll send you 6 more books, which you may either purchase at the discount price plus shipping and handling or return to us and cancel your subscription. *Terms and prices subject to change without notice. Prices do not include sales taxes which will be charged (if applicable) based on your state or country of residence. Canadian residents will be charged applicable taxes. Offer not valid in Quebec. Books received may not be as shown. All orders subject to approval. Credit or debit balances in a customer's account(s) may be offset by any other outstanding balance owed by or to the customer. Please allow 3 to 4 weeks for delivery. Offer available while quantities last.

If offer card is missing write to: Reader Service, P.O. Box 1341, Buffalo, NY 14240-8531 or visit www.ReaderService.com

BUSINESS REPLY MAIL

FIRST-CLASS MAIL PERMIT NO. 717 BUFFALO, NY

POSTAGE WILL BE PAID BY ADDRESSEE

READER SERVICE
PO BOX 1341
BUFFALO NY 14240-8571

screeching metal. The impact went on and on. Like a nightmare from which she couldn't wake up.

At last, it stopped. Everything stopped. Her heart was beating so hard, she thought she might throw up.

Gingerly, she lifted her head and straightened. The sirens she had anticipated wailed in the distance.

"Vaughn?" She reached for his hand, looking over toward him, and cried out. He had a gash on his forehead, and his face was dead white, his eyes glassy with shock.

"We're okay," he said automatically.

She squeezed his fingers. "Yes, we are. Hold on. Help is coming."

After that, time blurred, and the world went crazy.

Rescue personnel swarmed the plane, separating Vaughn and Brie in their haste to get them away from the smoldering wreckage. One set of EMTs worked on each of them in separate vehicles.

Brie waved away their concern with mounting frustration. "I'm fine. Seriously. Go see about Mr. Blackwood."

At last, they released her. She clambered out of the vehicle and ran across the rough ground to where Vaughn was still being evaluated. He smiled when he saw her, but the flash of white teeth lacked its usual wattage.

"Are you hurt?" he asked, his gaze sliding over her from head to toe.

"I'm fine. What are they saying about you?"

He shrugged. "A mild concussion. Couple of stitches. They don't want me to drive until tomorrow."

"So no meeting this afternoon?"

"It's important," he said. "I have to go. We'll grab a room near the club instead of staying at my place like I planned."

"I want to take care of you," she said.

He held out his hand. "Maybe we'll take care of each other."

Eleven

Vaughn lived in Fort Worth, but he was serving a term as vice president of the Dallas branch of the Texas Cattleman's Club. The clubhouse was where the big meeting and gala were to be held tonight. The two cities were half an hour apart, give or take. Under the circumstances, staying in the area made more sense than adding extra driving by going to Forth Worth just to come right back.

Brie nodded. "Sounds good." As the medics finished up their assessments, she watched Vaughn. His posture was *careful*, as if he was trying not to jostle anything that might give him pain. His head was surely the worst of his injuries.

"Does he need to go to the hospital?" Brie ignored

Vaughn's quick frown. Sometimes men could be stupid in these situations.

The male EMT gave her a reassuring grin. "It wouldn't hurt, but we couldn't get him to agree. Just be on the lookout for excessive drowsiness or any noticeable change. Garbled speech, sudden clumsiness. You know what I mean."

"Can he have painkillers?"

"As long as he's not driving, he could get his primary care physician to call something in."

Vaughn hopped down from the truck and took Brie by the arm. "Come on, Clara Barton. I told you. I'm fine." He thanked the team who had been working on him and then pulled out his phone. "I'm calling the car service I use. They'll pick us up at the terminal."

Brie was wearing heels. The ground was uneven. She wasn't dressed for hiking. "How do we get to the terminal?" she asked.

The same EMT waved a hand. "If you don't mind perching in the back, you can ride with us."

Fortunately, the firemen had determined the plane fuselage was stable, so they were able to retrieve Vaughn's and Brie's bags from the plane. Two carry-ons, two small suitcases.

The trip to the airport was quick. Brie and Vaughn sat side by side on the gurney, holding on to the metal edges as the vehicle bounced and lurched through the field. Behind them, the little plane lay crumpled and forlorn.

"What happens now?" she asked. "I'm assuming we don't simply walk away."

Vaughn shook his head and then cursed quietly when the motion clearly caused him pain. “We’ll have to deal with the FAA, but I don’t think it will take long. I have good insurance. They’ll file reports.” He paused and grimaced. “And we’ll have to book return tickets for tomorrow on a commercial flight.”

“I can deal with booking the return tickets while you’re tied up,” she said. Her heart still raced in her chest. They had come far too close to dying. A miscalculation on Vaughn’s part, no matter how small, could have spelled disaster.

She leaned her cheek against his shoulder. Now that the adrenaline was fading, she felt weak and shaky.

He curled an arm around her waist, his expression sober. “I’m sorry, Brie. I never meant to put you in harm’s way. I’ve flown thousands of miles in my own plane. But this was a rental. Never again. I should have known better than to trust someone else to maintain things properly.”

His words unsettled her. Not the part about the plane—nothing could be done about that. But the other part.

Vaughn had always kept his own counsel, gone his own way. He kept people at arm’s length, preferring to handle everything himself rather than count on anyone else. Even when he and Brielle had been sleeping together, he had given her his body, but not his heart and soul.

Despite her relative youth and inexperience at the time, she had recognized the difference.

Was he any better now at opening up? Did discovering he was a father do anything to loosen the tight control he kept over his emotions? She hadn't seen much evidence of a changed man.

Just minutes ago in the midst of a crisis, a near-fatal accident, Vaughn had kept his cool under pressure. If he had been scared, he hadn't shown it. While *Brie* had been sick with terror, Vaughn had simply done what had to be done.

That kind of mental focus in a critical situation was a great quality for a man to have while trying to save your life. He was the guy you counted on in an emergency. But she wanted more from him than superhero behavior. Maybe it was unfair, but she needed to know he could be vulnerable. Otherwise, he had no need for her at all other than sex. And a man could get that almost anywhere.

In the end, the FAA report was more than Vaughn had counted on. It was an hour before he and Brie were able to leave the airport. Despite his protestations to the contrary, Vaughn was *not* okay. After purchasing tickets—on Vaughn's credit card—to get them home tomorrow afternoon, she used the phone number he gave her to contact the transportation service he had summoned. The hired car had been waiting outside all this time.

After touching base with the driver, she scoped out the Cattleman's Club's location and booked rooms at a nearby hotel, an upscale chain that would be comfortable and quiet, two things she and Vaughn both needed after their traumatic morning.

When they exited the airport at last, Vaughn was

gray faced and exhausted. Brie took over quietly, ushering him into the car and speaking to the driver. She did the same thing at the hotel during check-in, dealing with the desk clerk and shielding Vaughn from annoying questions.

The bellman loaded their few bags onto a cart and escorted them upstairs. Vaughn extracted a $100 bill and thanked the young man. Then—when the door closed behind the jubilant kid—Vaughn shrugged out of his jacket and face-planted onto the mattress.

Brie shook her head in wry amusement. "At least take off your shoes," she said. "And tell me when we need to leave later. I'm not going to let you sleep more than thirty minutes at a time because of the possible concussion."

Vaughn lifted his head and glared. "I don't need a nurse."

"You need something," she said, putting a bite in her retort. "You look like hell, and you're getting mean. Either you cooperate with me, or I'll pull the plug on this meeting tonight."

Vaughn gaped. "You wouldn't. You couldn't."

She put her hands on her hips. "Try me."

To her utter astonishment, the man actually cooperated. Perhaps because he saw the sense in her words. Or more likely because he felt dreadful and arguing was too much of an effort.

He stood and stripped down to his shirt and knit boxers. Brie hadn't been prepared for how the sight of him half-naked would affect her. His legs were long and muscular and lightly dusted with hair. Vaughn was a gorgeous man in any situation. But right now, with his reserve temporarily at bay, she saw him as more approachable than usual.

Though she wanted to join him in the bed, she also wanted to feel clean again. She probably smelled of cornfield dust and antiseptic. "I'm going to take a quick shower," she said. "And wash my hair. Will you be okay?"

He had resumed his prone position. "Humph…" The guttural syllable was supposed to be an affirmative.

It bothered her to leave him, but surely the EMTs would have insisted on hospitalization if the head injury were dangerous enough that he couldn't be left unsupervised, even for a minute. With one last worried glance at the man sprawled on top of the covers, she grabbed her luggage and made her way to the bathroom.

Looking in the mirror was a mistake. Her face was milky pale, highlighting every bruise and scrape. She resembled somebody who had wrestled with an alligator and lost. Even the scratches on the side of her neck were unfamiliar.

Twenty minutes later, she was drying her hair and feeling hunger pangs. Because of the accident, they had forgotten to eat lunch. She thought about donning a hotel robe, but she needed more armor than that. It was far too early to dress for the evening, and her original outfit was crumpled and dusty.

Fortunately, she had thrown a pair of black yoga pants and an oversize turquoise T-shirt in her bag. When she was dressed and decent, with her hair twisted up in a neat knot on the back of her head, she checked on Vaughn again.

He had rolled onto his back at some point and now lay staring at the ceiling. His head turned when she walked into the bedroom. "Will you get me some acetaminophen?" he asked gruffly.

"Of course." Her heart clenched in sympathy. She knew that he hated asking for help. Instead of riffling through *his* things, she grabbed some tablets from her own toiletry case and brought him one of the complimentary water bottles from the mini fridge. "Do you feel like sitting up?"

Vaughn scowled. "Of course. It's a tiny cut with two stitches. That's all."

"Don't snap at me," she said calmly, handing him the meds and then the water. "You're the one determined to go out this evening. Couldn't we just go back to Royal?"

He swallowed the medicine and wiped his mouth, then ran his hands through his hair. "No. Because Cal McCready won't wait forever. I have a chance to get in on the ground floor of a land deal that could double or triple my business."

"But you're rich already. Why does it matter? There will be other deals, surely."

"These drilling rights are up for grabs, and I want them. McCready has convinced some old guy to sell a huge tract of land for an incredible price."

"McCready. I've heard that name. From you, I think. Didn't you tell me a long time ago that McCready was a snake?"

"I probably did. And he is. But don't worry. He won't

pull anything over on *me*. He wouldn't dare. Sometimes business makes strange bedfellows."

"I'm more concerned about the old guy than you. Are you sure McCready is on the up-and-up?"

"My head is killing me, Brie. I'm not really in the mood for a lesson in ethics from you."

"Fine," she said, her throat tight. "I'm going down to the lobby to buy a magazine."

"Wait," he muttered, reaching out to snag her wrist and bring it to his lips. He kissed the spot where her pulse thrummed visibly. "I'm sorry I snapped at you. Forgive me. This has been a hell of a day."

She allowed him to pull her down onto the bed, but she perched on the edge of the mattress instead of pressing against him. Both of them were upright. His fingers still encircled her wrist. It would be so easy to fall back into the covers and let nature take its course. Nothing mattered outside this room. It would be just the two of them, naked and needy.

Instead, she kept her spine straight and her impulses under control. "How about something to eat? Room service, not a restaurant." She spoke calmly, but being near him made her breath catch in her throat and her pulse accelerate.

They were so close, she could see the tiny dark lines of forest green that outlined the brighter irises so much like his daughter's sparkling emerald eyes.

"I could eat," he said.

He made no move to release her. Instead, he put a hand behind her neck and pulled her in for a kiss. It started out as light and playful, maybe meant to punctuate his apology. But in seconds, he had her panting and weak with wanting him.

Common sense said this relationship was going nowhere. Why else had the two of them not slept together every night they'd had a chance? They still weren't trusting each other enough to open up about what they really wanted.

Was he rethinking the faux engagement? He had never mentioned it after that first time. Brie told herself it was dumb to feel hurt, either for herself *or* for her daughter's sake.

Vaughn was who he was. Maybe this quick trip was a chance for Brie to get him out of her system once and for all. When they returned to Royal, she would break off even this tentative connection. Tell him that she and Danika didn't need him.

After all, no one believed Vaughn wanted to be a father. Least of all Brie.

All that aside, in this moment there was nowhere else she would rather be. He was big and broad and utterly male. Everything inside her yearned to get even closer.

Vaughn was the first one to pull back. He rested his forehead against hers, breathing heavily. "You're all clean, and I'm a mess," he said ruefully.

She gently touched the small bandage at the side of his forehead. "How does it feel?"

He rubbed a thumb over her bottom lip. "Sore. Manageable. I'll be fine." He hesitated. "I want you, Brie. More than anything. It makes me ill to think I might have hurt you, or worse."

"But you didn't," she said quietly. Because she

couldn't help herself, she ran her fingers through his thick, springy brown hair. "Go grab a shower if you want to. I'll have the food waiting when you get back. Steak? Chicken?"

His crooked grin was more like the old Vaughn. "A little bit of everything. I'm starving."

He took his bag and disappeared down the hall. Soon, Brie heard water running. It dawned on her then that he had never actually said when they needed to leave. Maybe he wasn't thinking clearly. She didn't want him to miss his oh-so-important meeting.

Though it was embarrassing, she knocked on the bathroom door, leaning a shoulder against the frame. "Vaughn? How much time do we have? I'm going to set an alarm so we won't be late."

The door opened so suddenly, she stumbled.

Vaughn hadn't gotten in the shower yet. His hair and his skin were still dry, but he was completely naked except for one of the hotel's plush towels he had wrapped around his hips.

His eyes sparkled with humor. "Did you decide to share?"

Her throat went dry. They were standing so close together she could have leaned forward and licked his collarbone. Heat radiated from his body. It was no wonder she had fallen in love with him all those years ago.

Whoa. No, no, no. She wasn't in love with Vaughn Blackwood. Maybe once upon a time when he was pursuing her hard and fast. But that was before their breakup. Before Danika. Before Brielle became a responsible mother to her child.

Not now...

Even as she voiced the mental denial, her hands reached for him. Placing both palms flat on his hard, sculpted chest, she ran her fingers up to his throat and then down to his navel…tracing ribs, tracking his heartbeat.

“Don’t take too long,” she muttered, not quite able to meet his mocking gaze. He knew exactly what he did to her.

Vaughn sucked in a sharp breath when she touched the edge of his towel. “Either stay or go, Brie, darlin’. Your choice. But make up your mind.”

Twelve

Vaughn cursed his own stupidity in giving Brie a choice. What he should have done was pull her into the shower with him for a long, leisurely round of hot, wet lovemaking. If he'd made the decision for them, he was sure she would have gone along with it. A man knew when a woman was interested.

What held him back was the knowledge that Brie was conflicted. He could see it in her eyes and in her body language. She wanted him. But she didn't *want* to want him. It was a fine distinction and one that unsettled Vaughn.

Unfortunately, her doubts mirrored his own. Why had he brought Brie with him to Dallas? The ostensible reason was to show her off as his new fiancée and let the gossip begin filtering back to Royal, so Miranda would find out.

However, that could have easily been accomplished without leaving town. The truth was, he needed to deal with this very important business meeting, and he wanted Brie by his side.

And then there was Danika. Those mornings when he drove her to day care had shown him that the beautiful child with the bright temperament was a delight. Any father would be lucky to have such a smart, curious kid. Did Vaughn even deserve to call her his own? He wasn't dad material. Again and again, he had asked himself if it wouldn't be better to let another—better suited—guy adopt the precocious little girl.

That was the part that stuck in his craw. He could almost convince himself that Nika was better off without Vaughn as a dad. But when he imagined Brie with another man, his blood pressure skyrocketed. Despite all evidence to the contrary, Brie was *his*.

His whole life he had always known how to get what he wanted. Years ago, when he was getting his business off the ground, he might even have stepped on people and things to meet his goals. He liked to think he had matured along the way, become more compassionate.

The careless arrogance he had evidenced as a twenty-five-year-old had altered and tempered. But he hadn't gone soft. Not at all. Which was why he was determined to make this enormous land deal with McCready happen.

He couldn't let himself be distracted by his need for Brielle.

Under the hot sting of the shower spray, he debated his options. She was the one question he couldn't answer, the one thorn in his flesh he was never able to excise.

Being intimate with her so soon after they reconnected in Royal had been a mistake. He knew that now. Sex complicated things, especially with a baby in the mix. But God, he couldn't bring himself to regret it.

His body hardened as he remembered that first incredible night. Never in a million years had he imagined that coming home for Sophie's wedding would end up with him in Brie's bed. The exhilaration of being inside her again had momentarily silenced all his discontent with his father's will and the drama with Miranda.

Making love to Brielle had seemed natural…inevitable.

But then morning had come, and with it, the harsh light of day. The inevitable voice of reason. Brielle was not the kind of woman a man picked up and put down when the mood struck him. She was decent and capable and kind. She had gone through nine months of pregnancy alone. Then she had spent two long years juggling the demands of a tiny baby, now a toddler… with no backup. No father to share the incredible load of parenting.

Vaughn could argue that it wasn't his fault. He hadn't known Danika existed. But the truth was more layered than that. If he hadn't been so adamant in the beginning that he didn't want anyone or anything to tie him down, Brie would never have broken up with him. She wouldn't have faced almost three years of unimaginable challenge without receiving any help or support from him.

Vaughn was culpable in that scenario, no matter how you sliced it. There were amends to be made.

Could he change? Was he willing to make the necessary sacrifices? He honestly didn't know. Even more daunting was the fact that he might not be who Brielle needed.

That last one was a gut punch.

As the water began to run cold, he washed his hair gingerly and then rinsed off, careful not to make contact with the bandage covering his stitches. He probably wasn't supposed to get the area wet, now that he thought about it.

Too late. His head had been killing him when the EMTs gave him instructions. He hadn't been thinking clearly.

With a glance at his watch, he realized that he was running out of time. Though he wanted to sprawl on the sofa and close his eyes, he went instead to his suitcase and pulled out his tux and neatly folded dress shirt.

When he appeared in the living room, Brie's eyes widened. "Wow," she said. "For a man who crashed a plane today, you look pretty darn great."

He sat beside her on the love seat and surveyed the plates of food. "It was a hard landing, not a crash," he said wryly. "Give me some credit."

For a moment, hunger took precedence over other considerations. He and Brie split the steak and ribs and baked chicken. Vaughn took the mashed potatoes. Brie chose the spinach salad, washed down with coffee.

When they were almost done, he curled a strand of her hair around his finger. "As much as I would love to stay here and goof off, we do have to leave in about twenty minutes. Does that give you enough time to get ready?"

Her eyes rounded, and her cheeks turned pink. "Next time, a little more warning would be nice."

He leaned over and kissed her softly, tasting the coffee on her lips. "You always look gorgeous. Throw on your fancy dress and some shoes, and you'll be good to go."

Slipping out of his arms, she stood and rolled her eyes. "Men. Glamour doesn't just happen. We have to work at it."

He chuckled as she disappeared down the hall, but humor was the last thing on his mind when she returned exactly eighteen minutes later, looking like a million dollars.

"Holy hell." He sucked in a breath.

Her face fell. "Too much? I asked Sophie what was appropriate. Was she wrong?"

How could Vaughn answer that question? "No," he said, his throat tight. "She wasn't wrong." On the other hand, Vaughn was not looking forward to other men seeing Brielle like this. She was stunning and sweet and drop-dead sexy.

The filmy white dress she wore was ethereal and sensual at the same time. Off the shoulder and fitted from breasts to knees, it almost made her appear to be naked. Because it was lined in a fabric that matched her skin tone, the whole effect was innocently suggestive. And sexy as hell.

Brie probably didn't even realize.

She wore the simple pearl necklace and earrings he had seen before. Her long, wavy blond hair was caught up in some kind of complicated knot, but with a few wispy pieces left loose to frame her face.

Turquoise eyes accented with mascara and smoky eye shadow turned his no-nonsense veterinarian into a femme fatale. Add spiky silver sandals and toes painted blush pink, and a man would be hard-pressed to decide where to start feasting on her.

He put his hands on her shoulders and massaged her soft skin, because he couldn't help himself. "You look beautiful, Brie. I'll be the envy of every man there. Let me message the driver, and we'll be on our way."

She smiled up at him, her excitement contagious. "It's been a very long time since I've had the opportunity to dress up and go out for an evening. An *adult* evening. Thanks for inviting me. I wasn't sure about leaving Danika, but I suppose there has to be a first time."

"My sister will spoil her rotten."

Brie chuckled. "I'm sure she will."

Vaughn found himself distracted during the brief drive to the TCC. Tonight was mostly about business, but that didn't keep him from anticipating the later parts of the evening when he and Brie would be alone together at the hotel.

She was the one who had made the hotel reservation while he was dealing with airport red tape. Since Brie had only booked the one room, she clearly hadn't changed her mind about them sleeping together. The realization made him hot and itchy.

His head still ached, but it would take far more discomfort than that for him to miss a chance to make love to this fascinating woman.

At the club, he was hailed as a conquering hero. Word about the forced landing had spread. People wanted to ask him about the experience.

Brie hung back as he fielded one conversation after another. She wasn't particularly shy, but everyone waiting to talk to him was male, not female. The club had accepted women as full members for some time now, but in many ways, it was still a man's world.

When there was a brief moment of privacy, Brie tugged on his arm. "What's the schedule?" she whispered.

"McCready has reserved a conference room from five until six. He's brought several of his board members."

"And what about you?"

"My lawyer is coming. But it's my company. I can negotiate on my own. Besides," he said, grinning, "I have you. My secret weapon. You'll dazzle and distract them, which will give me the edge."

Brie's lips twitched in amusement. "I'm sure I should be offended by that statement, but I'm feeling mellow, so I'll let it pass."

"Good." He curled an arm around her waist, inhaling her light perfume. "The gala officially starts at six thirty. They'll have heavy hors d'oeuvres and dancing. We can stay as long as we want…or we can head back to the hotel early."

As he watched, Brielle's face flushed dark pink. He loved that he could embarrass her so easily. She wasn't blasé about life, or anything else, for that matter. Being with her was fun. He'd never thought about it in those terms, but it was true.

They made their way down the central hallway to the back of the club and into the formal conference room. The decor relied on lots of polished wood and a traditional chandelier overhead. Cal was already in residence. His eyes widened when Vaughn walked in with Brie on his arm.

"Well, this is a surprise, Blackwood."

Vaughn lifted an eyebrow. "I'd like you to meet my good friend Brielle Gunderson. I thought she would enjoy the gala."

McCready was only a year younger than Vaughn, but he seemed older, because of the sleaze factor. The man wore Prada suits with lizard-skin loafers, an expensive cowboy hat and a killer smile that was supposed to disguise his cutthroat personality.

Brie was polite, but she didn't seem overly impressed. Vaughn relaxed inwardly. McCready wouldn't be above using a weapon against Vaughn, even if it meant dragging Brie into the middle of their business negotiation.

McCready had brought a team of six with him. Four men. Two women. One of the female VPs offered Brie a seat at the long oval table. Vaughn and his lawyer, Trent

Matthews—who arrived at the last moment—sat at the head with McCready.

After that, it was game on.

McCready leaned back in his chair. “I’ve got a big fish on the hook. He trusts me. I’m ready to move on this, but we need plenty of capital to seal the deal.”

“Money is not a problem,” Vaughn said calmly. “But I want to see everything in black-and-white before I make a decision.”

McCready smirked. “You don’t trust me, Blackwood?”

“I don’t trust anyone,” Vaughn said lightly, smiling deliberately to let everyone know he was kidding. Sort of… “When it comes to this many zeroes, it doesn’t pay to take unsubstantiated chances.”

Cal waved a hand at his VP of acquisitions. “Show Blackwood all your fancy charts and graphs.”

For the next half hour, conversation ebbed and flowed across the table. Vaughn didn’t entirely trust McCready, but in this instance, it did seem as if the time was ripe to snap up an unprecedented amount of land. The drilling rights alone were incredibly valuable.

No matter how impressed he was with the bottom line, Brie’s concerns rang in his ears. Was this a dirty deal? Or at the very least immoral?

Brie seemed content to watch and listen. At one point, though, he saw her ask a question of the woman sitting beside her. What was she thinking about all this?

Finally, Vaughn was satisfied he’d gotten all the information the others were willing to share. “You’ve given me plenty to consider, Cal. I won't stall. I'll have an answer for you in a week or so."

The workday was over, and the room emptied quickly except for the two men with the most to gain or lose. And Brie. She read the situation quickly. "If you'll excuse me, Vaughn," she said, "I need to make a phone call."

He knew she wanted to check on Danika. "Of course. Just come back here when you're done."

When the door closed behind Brie, Cal turned off the charm. "Fraternizing with the help again, I see. Isn't Gunderson the same little cookie who used to be your father's ranch hand? I always was envious of that revolving door to your bedroom."

Vaughn's temper boiled, but he kept his cool. "Shut up, McCready. We're here to talk business."

McCready shrugged. "Romantic entanglements can be *bad* for business. I'm not sure I like you bringing your lady friend to a private meeting."

The urge to punch the guy in the face was strong, but Vaughn reined in his fury. He would bide his time. There were other ways to get even with a snake. "Brie is my fiancée."

"I don't see a ring on her finger."

Cal's sneer was meant to enrage Vaughn, perhaps throw him off his game in the negotiations. And it almost worked. But with an effort, Vaughn tamped down his ire and kept his voice calm and even. "My personal life is not your concern, McCready. To be honest, you're one of the last people I'm interested in doing business with. But you seem to have something to offer, so I'm willing to play this out. For the moment."

"And that sweet piece of as—?"

Vaughn chopped the air with his hand. "Watch yourself, Cal."

Thirteen

Brie put a hand to her mouth, her stomach churning. As soon as she walked out of the room, she had remembered that her phone was in the pocket of her shrug sweater. But when she turned to go back in, she heard Cal McCready mention her name, so she froze and stayed just outside the partially open door.

They say eavesdroppers never hear good of themselves. That was certainly true today. She could understand McCready's crass statements. He was the kind of scumbag lowlife who somehow managed to stay just inside the fringes of polite society.

What was less understandable or pleasant was the fact that Vaughn hadn't exactly defended her honor.

He'd called her his fiancée, that was true, but he hadn't denied Cal's assessment of their past.

Should he have? Or did he believe that Cal McCready was not worth the effort?

The longer she stood there, the harder it was to contemplate going back into the room. She felt small and hurt inside. As if everything was different now. She had been so sure Vaughn was changing. Seeing him interact with Danika had made Brie believe money and success were no longer the driving forces in his life.

Maybe she was kidding herself.

Before she could summon the courage to walk into the conference room, the two men exited. Vaughn's smile warmed some of the cold edges of her soul. He handed over her shrug and phone. "There you are," he said. "I was about ready to send out a search party."

Cal's lecherous assessment of her face and figure made her feel unclean. Vaughn appeared not to notice.

"I think the gala has started," she said. "I hear music."

Vaughn turned his back on the other man. "I'll be in touch soon."

Brie sensed that Vaughn's careless dismissal made McCready furious, but rather than retorting, the other man spun on his heel and walked in the opposite direction. She was glad to see him go, though no less unsettled by the words that had been spoken. Vaughn's inner thoughts remained a mystery, unfortunately.

Vaughn took her arm and steered her toward the wing that housed the TCC ballroom. The party was already in full swing. Men in formal wear and women in gorgeous dresses crowded the food tables and filled the dance floor. A seven-piece orchestra played classics from the '40s and '50s.

The gala's theme was Blast From the Past. The planning committee had decorated the walls with vintage photographs, and some men had even come wearing old military uniforms.

It was fun and interesting, but best of all, there were plenty of romantic slow dances. Brie's toes tapped out a rhythm as Vaughn introduced her to one group of people after another…as his fiancée. Though she knew the ruse was for Miranda's benefit, Brie's heart jumped every time Vaughn said the words.

All of the people she met were cordial and respectful. After all, Vaughn was the current vice president of the club. Of course, there were more questions about the plane crash. Vaughn answered them all calmly, with good humor. But as she watched, she spotted the way Vaughn held himself just slightly aloof. A layer of reserve between him and everyone else.

Not arrogance in this situation. No desire to snub anyone. Just the slight postural discomfort that perhaps only Brie noticed.

At one point, Brie left him momentarily to make a call home. Sophie sounded happy and upbeat. Nika, about to go to bed, was cheerful, too, when Sophie held the phone so Nika could hear her mother. "I'll be home tomorrow, sweetie," Brie said. It was a useless reassurance. Kids that age had no sense of time. But it made Brie feel better as she returned to the party and found her date.

After talking to what seemed like hundreds of people, Vaughn led her to the buffet. They filled their plates with delicious appetizers and found a tiny table tucked away in a corner where they were able to eat without being disturbed.

For the first time that evening, Vaughn seemed to wilt visibly. She touched his hand. “Is your head bothering you?”

He scowled. “I’m fine.”

Men were such cranky patients. “You’re clearly *not* fine,” she said. “It’s been long enough since you took that last dose of medicine. Did you bring any with you?”

“No. I did not.” He cut into a bacon-wrapped scallop fiercely, as though the poor shellfish was to blame for what was likely a crushing headache.

“Oh, for heaven’s sake. Here,” she said, reaching into her small evening purse for the vial of ibuprofen she carried with her. “Your wound will only feel worse if you don’t stay ahead of the pain. To be honest, I’m sore, too, and I don’t have stitches in my skull.”

Vaughn’s head shot up. His expression turned to concern. “You don’t feel well?”

She grimaced. “A few twinges here and there. I think the seat belt is to blame for most of it. We hit the ground, Vaughn. There were bound to be consequences.”

Suddenly, that laser-like emerald gaze focused intently on *her*. “I see it,” he said, frowning. He touched her bare shoulder with a gentle fingertip. “I see the beginnings of a purple shadow. Why didn’t you tell me, Brie?”

“There’s nothing to tell. They checked me out after the accident. I’ll have a few bruises—nothing more. All I was trying to say is that you’re not any less of an alpha male if your head is bothering you. I know you’re probably tougher than most, but even you have limits. Here," she said. "We'll *both* take something. Is that less threatening to your masculinity?"

He downed the tablets with a swig of champagne. "Done," he said. "Are you satisfied? Let's hit the floor."

What he probably needed was rest, but she knew she wouldn't win that battle. "Sure," she said. "I'd love to."

For some reason, she didn't expect Vaughn to be a good dancer. Maybe because he wasn't a social animal. He proved her wrong in a big way. When he took her in his arms and slid into the music seamlessly, she was charmed and enchanted.

Vaughn held her like she was a princess. As he steered her around the room, he kept her tucked close to his chest. She could feel the thud of his heartbeat where her fingertips rested against the side of his neck. His warm breath brushed her ear.

Wearing her three-inch heels, she was only a few inches shorter than he was. They matched perfectly, every step in sync. It was magical and dangerous at the same time.

How could a woman not yearn to hang on to a man like this? Vaughn was her Prince Charming. Or she wanted him to be. She wasn't sure *what* Vaughn wanted.

One song led into another. Occasionally, someone would try to speak to them. Vaughn kept right on dancing, pretending not to hear or notice. Brie rested her cheek on his shoulder and smiled. She knew tonight was a fairy tale. Knew it wouldn't last.

Reality consisted of her job at the vet clinic and her small daughter, who had years of growing up to do with only her mother to raise her and care for her. Brie wouldn't be free to pursue her own selfish interests for a very long time.

Now that Danika was to be a flower girl, Brie and Vaughn would be enmeshed in wedding festivities for the upcoming week. But when Sophie's big day was over, there would be no more reason for Brielle to let herself be tempted by Vaughn Blackwood.

If Miranda was truly going to hand over money to Buckley's offspring, surely that would happen soon. If there was anything for Danika, great. Brie would invest it for her daughter. If not, that was fine, too. They'd get by without it. That was the easy part.

Sadly, for Brie, the bigger picture was becoming more clear every day. Vaughn's life and work were in the Dallas/Fort Worth area.

Though Vaughn had made an effort to come to Royal for his sister and was showing up for special events and supporting Sophie, he wouldn't be *staying* in Royal. He was committed to his other life, the one that didn't include Brie and Nika. That much was clear. Brie would only be courting more hurt and heartache if she let herself be persuaded otherwise.

Sometime later—time had ceased to matter—Vaughn nuzzled her cheek and whispered in her ear. "Are you ready to go back to the hotel, Brielle?"

She pulled back and looked up at him. Though he was not a hundred percent the old Vaughn, a naughty gleam in his eyes belied his bandaged head.

"I think that's a fabulous idea."

She had no idea how much Vaughn was paying his

car service, but the driver seemed to appear instantly anytime they were ready to go somewhere. Almost like a pumpkin carriage with tiny animated footmen. Brie could get used to this level of pampering.

Back at the hotel, shyness momentarily overtook her. She knew why *she* was indulging in this romantic overnight adventure. Her daughter was elsewhere, safely cared for. Brie was seizing the opportunity to feel like a woman again.

In her heart, she realized that this interlude with Vaughn had to be the end of any physical relationship. It was painful to contemplate, but she had no doubts. She was at peace with her decision.

If she had been weaving any dreams about him going down on one knee and declaring his undying love for her, the words she'd overheard at this afternoon's business meeting had put an end to that. Vaughn was a pragmatist. He was even willing to do business with a creep like Cal McCready if it meant a huge windfall for Blackwood Energy.

No doubt, Vaughn's fake engagement ploy was more of the same dispassionate, expeditious behavior of a calculated businessman.

He ushered her into their room and locked the door. Then he loosened his bow tie and pulled it free of his collar. As he struggled with the button at his throat, Brie moved closer. "Let me," she said huskily. He smelled amazing. She'd been enjoying the crisp scent of starched cotton and citrusy aftershave all evening.

He froze when she went toe-to-toe with him, invading his space. She saw his tanned throat flex as he swallowed. "I could have done it myself," he muttered.

She freed the stubborn button and moved on to two more and then two more after that. Soon, she was ready to lift his shirttail from his pants. His taut abdomen was warm and hard beneath her curious fingertips. "I'm happy to help," she said, kissing the center of his chest and drawing his shirt upward from his belt. "After all, you saved my life today."

He chuckled hoarsely. "I was technically the one who put you *in* jeopardy, so I'm not going to brag about the whole savior thing. For the record, though, the FAA thinks it was likely an engine malfunction."

"Maybe I should be in charge tonight…you know… since you've been injured."

His green eyes flashed with heat. "I'm listening."

"Think about it," she said. "In the old days, you always called the shots. I was naive about men when I met you. I suppose I could say you taught me everything I know."

"You weren't a virgin."

"No. Did that bother you?"

"Of course not. I don't believe in double standards."

"Still, you were light-years ahead of me in experience."

"Did that bother *you*?" He threw the question back at her, his expression hard to read.

"Sometimes," she admitted. "I knew I was the flavor of the week. You had a reputation. Still have one, I guess. There were a lot of women giving me the death stare tonight. I couldn't tell them you weren't really off the market."

"As long as we're engaged, even if it's a faux engagement, I won't do anything to dishonor you, Brie. You have my word."

"Thank you. Hopefully, this arrangement will be resolved before long. If Miranda is about to spring a few surprises about the estate, I think it will be soon. Her life is in New York now. She's already spent far longer settling your father's affairs than most people thought she would. I heard that Buckley made a huge donation to her charity."

"Probably the only decent thing he ever did."

The shadows in his eyes bothered her. "It's okay to love people, Vaughn, even when they disappoint us. Your father had his faults, plenty of them, in fact. But you loved him. I know you must have been grieving in your own way."

He rested his forehead against hers. "Mostly, I've been angry. At him. At Miranda. At myself."

She cupped his cheek, feeling the late-day stubble, the warm skin. "Why yourself?"

Vaughn pulled free and crossed the room, pausing to stare out the window at the twinkling lights of Dallas. Their suite was on the top floor. Brie had requested a simple king room. The hotel had upgraded them after she'd given Vaughn's name.

He leaned his forearm against the glass and sighed. "I was a punk-ass adolescent. Even if he had wanted to be a good father, I made sure he knew I didn't need him or anybody. And once that distance between us was in place, it stuck."

"You're feeling guilty because he died alone." She made it a statement. Vaughn didn't deny her claim.

Instead, he searched out a bottle of wine and released the cork, pouring two glasses and handing Brie one. "Enough serious talk," he said. "We came here to have fun."

She wrinkled her nose. "I thought you came to make a deal with Cal McCready."

"You don't approve?"

"It's not my place to approve or disapprove. But if you're asking my opinion, the man gives me the creeps."

"Fair enough. I probably shouldn't have taken you to that meeting. I'm sorry, Brie."

"It wasn't bad. I was intrigued. It was my first opportunity to see you in your natural habitat."

The corners of his mouth ticked up in a rueful grin. "My natural habitat? I think I've been insulted."

She drained her wineglass and kicked off her shoes, groaning when her bare toes dug into the plush carpet. "Not at all. I thought you were very sexy. Everyone in the room hung on your every word. It must be a kick to have so much power."

He set his glass aside, still half-full. "You should know, Brie. You've always had that kind of power over me. In the bedroom."

She gaped at him. "That's absurd."

"Is it?" He stood there, cocky as hell with his bare chest and his ruffled hair, and gave her an emerald-eyed look that sent heat coursing through her lower abdomen.

"Why are you teasing me?" she stuttered.

He reached for her hand and dragged her close. "It's called foreplay, my sweet Brie. I'm surprised you haven't heard of it."

Fourteen

Vaughn had always enjoyed sparring with Brielle Gunderson. But not as much as making love to her. If he hadn't been hard as an iron pike, he might have been amused by her slack-jawed astonishment. Under the circumstances, he didn't enjoy winning this round as much as he should have.

"Kiss me, Brie," he said. "Like you mean it."

Her lashes lowered, hiding her expression. But her lips met his without hesitation. There it was again. The jolt. The blow. The all-out shock to his system.

He lifted her off her feet and shoved his mouth on hers roughly. His plan had been to woo her, to coax her into giving him her trust, her hunger, her soft woman's body.

Instead, he lost his mind. "How does this damn dress come off?" he groaned.

Brie leaned into him, arms encircling his neck. "Over my head. It's stretchy. You know..."

He did *not* know. But he was about to find out.

Releasing her was an effort. He made himself set her on her feet. "Lift your arms," he said as he grabbed the hem of her skirt.

She obeyed, but as he dragged the fabric to her hips and higher, he floundered. Her tiny panties revealed everything. And his lover wasn't wearing a bra. Because the dress was two thin layers instead of one, he hadn't noticed. He must be slipping.

Now Brie was naked from her toes to her neck, except for a tiny scrap of nylon at her hips. Her voice was muffled. "I'm suffocating," she complained.

He had unwittingly stopped short of pulling the dress off completely, gobsmacked by the sight of Brie's naked body. Most of the dress was swathed around her head. "Sorry," he muttered. He kept at it, and moments later, tossed the dress aside.

"My hair's a mess now," she said.

Vaughn took her hands and lifted them one at a time to his lips. As he kissed each palm, he inhaled sharply, feeling his chest wobble in a weird way. "You're perfect."

Slowly, he removed all the hundred and one pins holding her artful hairstyle together. Then he winnowed his fingers through her silky blond tresses until they fell across her bare shoulders.

Brie put her hands over his. "Make love to me, Vaughn."

"Yes." The single syllable was guttural. It was hard to talk with a boulder in his throat.

He scooped her up and carried her to the bed. Brie looked at him so intently it made him nervous. "What?" he said, sprawling beside her. "Why are you looking at me like that?"

She shrugged with a small smile on her lips. "I like looking at you. But I notice you're still wearing pants."

He glanced down, surprised to see that she was right. "Maybe I do have a concussion," he said ruefully. Or maybe he was distracted because he was suddenly coming to realize just how much Brie meant to him. He couldn't tell her. Not yet. Not when he didn't understand it himself.

"Five seconds," he promised, stumbling to his feet and removing the rest of his clothing.

"And not to be picky," she said, "but I'm really hoping for more than one condom."

"Duly noted." He'd taken care of that item back in Royal before he did anything else for this trip.

When he joined her a second time, he pulled her close, burying her face in his shoulder and inhaling the scent of her shampoo. He ran his hands down her back, stopping when he reached the tantalizing curves of her cute butt.

Brie stirred restlessly. "You're smothering me again."

He pulled back and chuckled. How could he be so aroused and yet feel such an enormous wave of emotion for this woman? "I think I've lost my mojo," he said, not entirely kidding. Knowing that she could have died today affected him deeply.

"Because of the bump on your head?"

"That could be it." Or more likely, he was navigating unknown territory. This *thing* with Brie was about more than sex. His gut tightened. He'd never admitted that, even if it was true three years ago. When she walked out on him—because he pushed her away—he'd been devastated.

But his attitude at the time had been *to hell with women, this one in particular.* He'd buried himself in his work and convinced his heart (if he had one) that he was better off without her.

For almost three years, he had believed the lie. Right up until the moment Brie showed up on Sophie's doorstep.

And now he had a daughter.

The whole situation was a huge, tangled train wreck.

But now was not the moment to look for solutions. Now was the chance to play.

He took his time with her. There was no one knocking at the door, no urgent phone calls. Danika was safe and happy with Sophie. Vaughn was free to make Brie as insane with hunger and desire as she made him.

She was on her back now. He leaned over her, resting his weight on one elbow. Big aquamarine eyes scanned his face. The uncertainty he sensed in them shamed him. No wonder she was not entirely comfortable with this relationship. He had never given her any reason to think he was a guy who could be counted on to stand beside her and make a real commitment.

But a man could change. His sister believed it. Dixie,

too. Slowly, Vaughn was coming to understand that perhaps he wasn't as much of an independent loner as he had once thought.

He kissed her forehead, her nose, her delicate throat, each pert raspberry nipple. "Tonight was fun," he said. "We should do it more often."

"The club gala was great." She paused. "I can't do this kind of thing on a regular basis, though. I like spending time with you, Vaughn, but it's complicated and messy. I'm at a point in my life where I need structure and stability. Let's concentrate on the here and now."

Her speech winded him, nicked his pride. Did she not even want to try anymore?

"Carpe diem," he whispered, bending his head to find the vulnerable indentation below her ear. When Brie whimpered and arched her back, he exulted. *This* he was good at. This he could do.

He spent the next half hour worshipping every inch of her creamy, smooth skin. No tiny spot went unnoticed.

Brie begged. She moaned. She pleaded.

He had wanted her for so long now, his unappeased erection might do him in. Crippled with lust and blinded by the need to make her admit how much she wanted and needed him, he drove her higher and higher, using every trick in his arsenal.

When he kissed her again, she bit his lip. Hard. Enough that he tasted the tang of blood on his tongue. He jerked back. "Hell, woman. What was that for?"

"Quit torturing me. I want you inside me. Now."

Her urgency sent his arousal an impossible notch higher. He rolled off the bed so fast he nearly landed on his head. While Brie had the audacity to giggle, Vaughn located the protection and waved a strip over the bed. "Think this will do it?"

Brie pretended to consider the question seriously, trying not to grin. "Maybe for the first hour."

After that, things blurred. Vaughn rolled on protection, not waiting for Brie to help. He didn't even let her touch him. He was so wired that any little bit of stimulation from her was going to flip his switch.

Instead, he moved between her thighs, spread them farther and tried to catch his breath. He entered her slowly, bracing himself on his elbows to spare her his full weight. She seemed precious to him. Fragile. When he reached the head of her womb, they both sighed in unison, as if they had made it through dangerous waters to a final destination.

But Vaughn was just beginning. Brie's body was tight and warm, wrapping him in incredible heat, caressing his sex with inner muscles. He withdrew once, intending to stroke slowly, again and again, until he made her come.

Instead, Brie locked her ankles behind his back and canted her hips. "Harder," she pleaded. "More."

That did it. He snapped. If she wanted harder, he could oblige. The bed shook as he thrust wildly. Brie cried out his name.

Dimly, he realized she was climaxing. He wanted to pause and appreciate her excitement, but his own orgasm slammed into him and yanked him into a dark place where pleasure was so overpowering that it bordered on pain. He groaned aloud, shuddering at the intense release.

Then exhaustion claimed him, and he let oblivion roll over him.

At 3:00 a.m., Brie shifted and looked at her phone. Her legs ached, her sex was tender and she had a goofy smile plastered all over her face. Thankfully, it was dark and there was no one around to see.

No one but Vaughn, and he was still dead asleep. Her inventive, flatteringly desperate lover had rocked her world and then collapsed. She was vaguely worried about his head, but surely no one that virile and *accommodating* could be seriously hurt.

Gingerly, she slid out of bed. After using the bathroom, she washed up—everywhere—and examined her reflection in the mirror. Some of her aches and pains were from the plane crash. The bruise on her shoulder was turning a darker shade of purple.

The idea of boarding a jet later today made her slightly queasy, but she knew waiting would only make the fear worse. Instead of thinking about what was to come, she returned to the bedroom and scooted back under the covers.

The air-conditioning had chilled her skin. Spooning Vaughn's big, warm body was like huddling up to a campfire. Instant bliss.

He mumbled something. She stroked his hair. "Go back to sleep."

* * *

Vaughn had set an alarm. It was a good thing, because he and Brie were sound asleep when the damned phone went off. He silenced the annoying chirp and groaned.

Sometime before dawn he had awakened and found a soft, sleeping woman beside him. It wasn't long before he was making love to Brie. Again.

Then more blissful sleep. When was the last time he'd had such a restful night? Maybe never.

He was starting to get the idea that he might want to sleep like this forever.

He turned on his side and faced her. There was just enough ambient light to see her features outlined in shadow. Her lashes were dark crescents on her cheeks.

"Brie. Wake up, sweet thing."

She mumbled and buried her head in the pillow. He grinned. Though Brie was accustomed to getting up early every morning with a busy toddler, she *wasn't* in the habit of being disturbed during the night by a hungry male in her bed.

"I've got a meeting with my lawyer at nine thirty," he said quietly. "It won't take long. Just a few loose ends so he and I are on the same page. This deal with McCready may need to be tied up while I'm still in Royal."

"Mm-hmm." Still her eyes were closed.

"Checkout isn't until noon. I'll be back in plenty of time."

One arm raised. She waved a hand. "Go. I'll order room service. Don't worry about me."

He rolled out of bed. "If you order in a hurry, I'll eat with you. But I have to be out of here in forty-five minutes."

Vaughn had a hard time concentrating on business. The vision of a sleepy Brie wrapped in a hotel robe eating strawberries was a hard one to shake. He'd had twelve minutes to wolf down an omelet and a flaky croissant before he'd had to run. He'd taken his coffee in a to-go cup in the car.

His lawyer, Trent Matthews, was droning on now about something. The man was two decades older than Vaughn. They had different outlooks on life. Vaughn should probably have found other representation long ago, but his father had fired Trent way back when, and Vaughn had felt sorry for the man.

The guy wasn't a bad lawyer. The women certainly seemed to like him. The charming, aging Brad Pitt type, still had influence in the Dallas/Fort Worth area, so he had more going for him than looks.

Vaughn focused on the task at hand. "Are we clear how to proceed with McCready?"

"Sure," Trent said heartily. "Where do things stand on your father's will? Have you thought about challenging Miranda Dupree in court?"

Matthews was definitely overstepping. Vaughn kept his cool. "There *is* a slight possibility that things aren't final yet. And you should know that my fiancée and I have a daughter together. I plan to pursue any possible share of my father's inheritance for my daughter's sake. She's currently Buckley's only grandchild."

Trent blanched. “I see. Well, then, I can amend these documents.”

Vaughn scowled, feeling his skin crawl in warning. “What documents, Matthews?”

The lawyer didn’t meet his gaze. Instead, he shuffled piles on his desk. “When I heard yesterday that you were engaged, I drew up some papers to protect you in this deal we’re working on. Not a prenup, per se. Simply an acknowledgment that Ms. Gunderson is not entitled to any of the proceeds from the McCready deal, because it was already in process before she became your fiancée. Pretty standard stuff. In case you were to marry and divorce. Look for yourself.”

Vaughn took the papers automatically, his brain spinning. He perused the sheaf of legalese with growing distaste. According to this, Brie would be cut out even *when and if* she and Vaughn were married.

He handed them back. “Why in the hell would you do this without asking me? My wife will be entitled to everything I own. No. A thousand times no.”

Trent’s gaze widened. “Because I didn’t put the kid in yet?”

Vaughn’s glare was furious. “The *kid’s* name is Danika. Whatever I have is hers. You can shred all of that, Matthews. I don’t need it.”

As Vaughn stormed out of the building, sick to his stomach and incredibly frustrated, he recognized this watershed moment for what it was. He’d spent his entire career making decisions based on the financial bottom line…putting money before relationships.

Those days were gone. No matter what happened

between Brielle and him, he was no longer capable of being an island. A man with a daughter had to change.

Whether he liked it or not…

Fifteen

Brie put Sophie's call on speakerphone and continued loading the dishwasher. Danika played at her feet. "I don't know why you're so upset, Sophie. You went to England. Shrewsbury Hall, right? These people aren't strangers."

Sophie voice quavered. "You don't understand. This is different. Nigel's family has never been to Royal. He and I are going to walk into the Bellamy and watch British aristocracy go smack up against Texas cowboy culture. Tea cozies and mechanical bulls. Centuries of history and culture versus twenty-four-ounce steaks and silver-dollar bars."

Brie laughed in spite of Sophie's distress. "And to make matters worse, under the roof of that same five-star resort are four reality TV actresses." Who, as everyone in Royal knew, were Miranda's larger-than-life costars from *Secret Lives of NYC Ex-Wives*, all back for the wedding.

Brie dried her hands and picked up the phone. "Relax, Soph. Talk to Nigel if you're freaking out. I'm sure there won't be *actual* bloodshed." When she hung up a few moments later, she was still chuckling.

Brie was really excited about Sophie's wedding. What woman didn't enjoy the spectacle of a huge ceremony with an enormous crowd of well-wishers? She had taken Danika to Natalie Valentine's bridal shop and had her fitted in the adorable flower girl outfit Sophie had selected. Plenty of eyelet lace and grosgrain ribbon and ruffles.

Nika loved her new costume, even if she didn't fully understand what was to come.

Vaughn had been curiously quiet and withdrawn on their return to Royal. Perhaps he was being careful to protect Brie's reputation by not staying at her house overnight. Some folks in Royal were pretty conservative. While she appreciated his courtesy and circumspection, she missed him desperately.

His reticence was aligning with Brie's plan to end their sexual relationship. She should be happy. But she hadn't expected it to hurt quite so much.

Still, life was too busy to dwell on what might have been. Because Nika was in the wedding, Brie was now on the guest list for the rehearsal dinner. Which meant finding a dress for that occasion *and* the wedding. She had planned to wear something already in her closet, but while she'd been at the bridal shop, Natalie had pulled out all the stops and talked Brie into two entirely new outfits that were too beautiful to pass up.

Brie's credit card took a hit, but with her childcare costs reduced, she could afford to splurge. Though it was humbling to admit, she wanted Vaughn to see her in her new dresses. She wanted him to know what he was missing.

Sophie and Nigel must have been living right. The weather forecast for the wedding weekend called for blue skies, warm temps and low humidity. The excitement in Royal was off the charts. It wasn't often that an actual English dame showed up.

Not that Nigel's grandmother was stuffy at all. Brie had met her briefly. The elderly lady was quite a character. And she certainly didn't stand on ceremony.

Closer to home, Brie and Vaughn had argued over the schedule for Friday afternoon and evening. Brie thought Vaughn ought to be out at Blackwood Hollow ranch to help his sister and the rest of the family with any last-minute emergencies that might arise.

Vaughn stood in her living room and scowled. "You and Nika should come with me. No sense in having two vehicles. Parking is going to be a zoo."

Brie held on to her patience by a thread. She was exhausted already, and Vaughn was still not acting like himself. "Believe me," she said. "The important thing is to make sure that Danika is in good shape for the wedding. Two-year-olds have a narrow window of cooperative behavior in situations like a wedding rehearsal. My plan is to give her a late nap and then drive her out there just in time for the wedding director to start lining everyone up."

Vaughn shook his head slowly. "It's only throwing a few rose petals from a basket. How hard can it be?"

She went to him and touched his arm. "This will be a stressful day for everyone. Trust me on this, Vaughn. Please."

He exhaled. "Okay. But I don't like it. I wanted everyone to see us together."

"And they will," she said. "But we're not going to be the focus. This weekend is all about your sister, the bride."

His handsome mouth quirked in a smile. "As if she would let either Kellan or me forget it." He paused. "Nigel is a good guy—right? I want Soph to be happy."

"I think he's wonderful. You're gaining a brother-in-law who will be very good to her. I can already tell. He dotes on Sophie. Surely you've noticed."

"I have," he admitted. "It's sickeningly cute."

"Don't be such a cynic. Love makes the world go round, haven't you heard?"

"I'm not sure I know what love is. Do you?" He shocked her with a serious answer.

The room fell silent. Nika was only a few feet away happily playing with her building blocks.

Brie swallowed. Maybe now was the time to let Vaughn know that it was okay to live his life on his own terms. "I think love means letting the other person be who they are. Love isn't love if you're always trying to change someone. When two people are in love, they should care more about their partner's happiness than their own." She paused self-consciously. "I guess that's more than you wanted to know."

His gaze was guarded. Intense. "Not at all. I think it makes perfect sense. And I'll bow to your wisdom about Danika. You're her mother. You know her best."

"Thank you for understanding."

He glanced at his watch. "In that case, I suppose I should head on out to the ranch. I'll take other clothes with me and shower at the bunkhouse. Kellan and I have volunteered for manual labor. I don't know if Darius has arrived yet."

Brie followed him to the door. "And it wouldn't hurt to keep an eye on Nigel's family. They're great, but a bit overwhelming with the lot of them all together. Sophie's intimidated, I think. Let her know you're in her corner."

Vaughn curled an arm around her and tugged her in for a quick but thorough kiss. "You're a good person, Brie."

His unexpected affection caught her off guard. She would have been happy to linger over the kiss, but Vaughn was already on the way out the door.

"I'll see you soon," she said.

He turned, with the sunlight grazing his masculine profile. "Call me if you need me. I mean it, Brie. I want you to enjoy tonight. You deserve a pleasant evening, even if you are the mother of the flower girl. You work hard. It's time for some play."

Kace LeBlanc was suffering from wedding fever. He was as surprised as anyone to find out he was susceptible. It didn't help that his office was near Natalie

Valentine's bridal shop. Every time he glanced out the window, he was treated to a view of women and girls parading in and out, excitedly choosing finery for the wedding of the season.

Considering the fact that only months ago the entire Blackwood family was in a deep funk, it was nothing short of miraculous that at least two of them had found happiness. First Kellan, now Sophie.

The weddings made Kace feel a little less guilty.

To be honest, he was tired of being considered the town scrooge just because he was one who'd delivered the bad news about a certain controversial will. He had a job to do, and he did it well. It wasn't his fault that the dead sometimes left chaos in the wake of their passing.

Buckley Blackwood had certainly put his kids though the wringer. And left a mess for his personal lawyer and his ex-wife to negotiate. Kace sometimes wanted to get his forehead tattooed—*Don't shoot the messenger.*

At the moment, though, his professional life wasn't the problem. Kace was horny. And confused. And about to do something utterly un-Kace-like.

Even worse, he had no idea at all how Lulu was going to respond. They had never talked about getting serious. Or even about being a couple, for that matter. The TV star had dazzled him from the moment he met her, early on when *Secret Lives* first began filming in Royal. But their relationship had not exactly gone smoothly.

He patted his pocket and pulled up the daily calendar on his phone. Timing was everything. Kace had been forced to bribe one of the *Secret Lives* cameramen in order to pull off this coup. The fact that the outcome was uncertain left his stomach in a knot.

When he checked his watch, he saw that it was eleven forty-five. In exactly fifteen minutes, Lulu Shepard and three of her costars were supposed to meet at the Royal Diner, have lunch and then head over to Natalie's to pick up their gowns for the wedding tomorrow.

Kace was planning a rendezvous.

He stared down the street, remembering the day he and Lulu first met. It was last December. The entire town had been decked out in Christmas finery. Kace hadn't been feeling any particular holiday spirit, but his office was being painted, so he had camped out in the diner with legal papers spread all over his table.

In swooped one of the most beautiful and appealing women he had ever seen. He'd noticed her warm brown skin and wild, glorious hair immediately. Her deliberately provocative personality had taken time to warm up to.

The infuriating woman had sassed him and made fun of him and generally driven him up the wall at their first meeting.

But she had made an impression. Lord help him, Lulu Shephard had burst into his life like a whirlwind, and he hadn't been the same since. Half the time he wanted to smack her. The other half he was mad with lust for her curvaceous, sexy body.

What was a highly trained legal mind supposed to do with that conundrum?

At exactly eight minutes before twelve, he shut off

his laptop and stood to fasten the top button of his shirt and straighten his tie.

His palms were sweaty. His heart raced. There was no going back from this. When his nerve nearly failed him, he summoned an image of Lulu in his bed… screaming, as she had once promised him in jest. Hearing her groan his name when she came was one of the highlights of his life.

Hell. His body tightened. It was too late to remember that he needed a haircut. In an ill-fated attempt to tame his rumpled look, he scraped two hands through his hair.

By the time he made it to the diner, his forehead was damp. Couldn't blame the weather. It was Kace who was a mess.

He was a very private man as a rule. Lulu lived her life, at least for the moment, under the ever-watchful eye of the cameras. Being a reality TV star meant little privacy during the day.

Thankfully, there had been zero witnesses when Kace had taken her to bed. Not that he was ashamed of what they were doing. Oh no. But certain things were sacred between a man and a woman. To his relief, Lulu had been equally discreet, working with him to hide their rendezvous from the ever-present cameras that followed her everywhere.

As he opened the door of the diner, he met the gaze of the cameraman, Sam, who was already set up to film the women as they entered the eatery. His cohort, Henry, would be bringing up the rear of the group, so there would be plenty of different shots to build an episode.

Sam grinned and gave Kace a thumbs-up.

Kace managed to nod and tried not to puke. He hated the limelight. This entire endeavor was supposed to show his luscious Lulu that he was meeting her on her terms.

The regular folks in the diner had obviously perked up when they saw Sam. You would think after all this time that Royal's citizens would be sick of having snippets of their lives show up on TV, but they all seemed to be enjoying the notoriety, even now.

The door swung open, and the cameras started to roll. Rafaela was first, of course. She was invariably intent on capturing the most screen time. Her raison d'être was fame, and her biggest concern was how the *Secret Lives* show was going to propel her to the big-time.

Next was party girl Zooey, and then Seraphina, who was Lulu's best friend and the fiancée of local rancher and former war hero Clint Rockwell. Kace had briefly entertained bringing Fee in on the secret, but she and Lulu were tight. He wasn't sure the other woman could keep quiet.

Miranda was the only ex-wife missing. She had been kind of busy lately with real-life drama.

Finally, the woman he wanted to see breezed in. She was wearing tight black leather pants, five-inch stilettos and a tangerine sweater that emphasized her bountiful breasts.

Kace was hard instantly.

When she saw him, her ever-ready confidence faltered. “Kace. What are you doing here?” She stepped in front of him, obviously trying to shield him from the cameras.

He slid his hands beneath her hair, tilted her head to one side and put his lips on hers, tasting the seam of her mouth, probing for entry. When he’d kissed her quite thoroughly, he finally pulled back. “Hi,” he said huskily.

Lulu was completely thrown off stride. She pulled back and glanced over her shoulder, making a slashing motion with one hand, telling the cameras to stop rolling. Sam and Henry ignored her.

Her gorgeous almond-shaped eyes widened as Kace grabbed her a second time.

“I haven’t seen you in two days,” he complained. “I’ve missed you.”

Lulu melted into him for a full thirty seconds, moaning quietly as he let her know how *much* he had missed her. But this time she broke free, agitated now.

“They’re filming us,” she hissed urgently. “Let’s slip out the back, and we can talk.”

“I don’t want to slip out the back,” Kace said stubbornly. “It doesn’t matter who’s watching.” One glance told him that Sam and Henry were ready.

Kace went down on one knee and pulled a sapphire velvet box from his pocket. He flipped open the lid, exposing the large, flawless solitaire he had picked out. “Lulu Shephard, will you marry me?”

A unison gasp swept around the diner. Lulu’s costars uncharacteristically held back from displaying any drama, their expressions wobbling between awe and envy and delight.

Lulu put her hands to her cheeks, tears glistening, threatening to spill over. "Are you crazy?" she whispered. "You're a by-the-book lawyer. I'm a reality TV star."

He got to his feet, still holding the box. "Don't cry, Lu, my sweet girl. You'll ruin your makeup." Using his fingertip, he gathered her tears carefully and wiped them on his pants leg. "This is our big moment. Editing can only do so much," he chuckled.

Lulu sucked in a breath. "I can't believe you're doing this, especially right now."

"Romance is in the air this weekend," he said. "I wanted in on the excitement. Lulu, my love, you're the piece of my life I never knew was missing. You make me laugh. You make me want your insanely hot body. You make me proud to know you. Say you'll marry me, Lulu. Say you'll be my wife till death do us part. Say you want me, too. Please."

From a few feet away, Fee's excited voice called out encouragement. "Say yes, Lulu. Do it."

Everything in the room blurred and went still. All Kace could see was his lover's face. "Do you love me, Lulu? Will you wear this ring and make me a happy man?"

His larger-than-life, vulnerable-beneath-the-surface sweetheart wiggled her hand in front of his face. "Yes, yes, yes!" she cried. "Oh my gosh, I'm engaged." Her beaming smile could have powered a small city.

Kace slipped the beautiful ring on the third finger of her left hand. He leaned close to her ear, dropping his voice so that even the powerful mics couldn't eavesdrop on his words. "No take-backs, Lulu. This is for now and for always. I'm never letting you go."

When she kissed him, he forgot the cameras were recording. He forgot he liked an orderly, dignified life. Everything he had ever wanted was right here in his arms.

According to the networks, there was no such thing as too much good TV, but eventually, the diner manager cleared his throat loudly. "Um, break it up, you two. We've got customers waiting on their orders."

Kace and Lulu stepped back from each other sheepishly and grinned. Her smile faltered. "I love you, too, Kace. I'm sorry I said lawyers lacked a sense of humor and had no talent for joy in their lives. I was wrong."

"Actually," he muttered, "you didn't say that about *all* lawyers…just me."

"Oh, lordy." Her expression was mortified. "Are you always going to remember every mean thing I say?"

"Probably. But don't worry, sweetheart. You can make it up to me later. In bed," he clarified, just in case she wasn't paying attention.

One of the townspeople shouted encouragement. "Kiss her again, LeBlanc."

"Don't mind if I do…"

Sixteen

Brie looked in the rearview mirror to make sure Danika was doing okay. Of all days, Nika had chosen today to nap longer than usual. Brie was forced to wake her up at four, which was guaranteed to put her daughter in a grumpy mood.

Now, the little girl had a sippy cup of water and a bag of animal crackers in her lap and seemed to be content, at least for the moment. The rehearsal was at six. Which meant Nika's dinner would be late. Brie was trying to ward off a meltdown.

When they got to Blackwood Hollow, Brie followed directions Vaughn had sent in a text. Two huge white tents stood against the indigo of an early-evening sky. One was set up for the rehearsal dinner, the second for the ceremony itself—hundreds of chairs and a very long center aisle.

Brie had her doubts about being able to coax her daughter all the way to the front, much less throw petals the way she was supposed to, but Sophie was dead set on having her niece play a part, so whatever happened would happen.

One glance at her watch told Brie she had timed her arrival as closely as possible. She lifted the hatch of her little car, stripped Danika down in the back and quickly dressed her in a cute, comfortable sundress. Sophie's wedding director would have the basket of rose petals. Fake ones for tonight, and the real deal for tomorrow.

Vaughn met her at the back of the tent. His shoulders visibly relaxed at the sight of them. "I was getting worried."

"We're here," she said, squeezing his hand.

He bent to pick up Danika. "How's my little girl?"

As Brie watched, openmouthed, Nika cuddled up to Vaughn's shoulder and giggled when he pretended to tickle her tummy. Father and daughter had been spending time together, but Vaughn hadn't been by the house in several days. Brie was surprised by her daughter's openness. Pleasantly so.

Sophie joined them, vibrating with excitement. "We're about to start. Do I look okay?"

Vaughn kissed his sister's cheek. "You look gorgeous. Is everyone here?"

"One of the groomsmen is on a delayed flight, but we have a stand-in."

The director scurried over. “Ms. Blackwood? I’m ready if you are.”

After that, it was controlled chaos. The bridesmaids and groomsmen practiced processing in and walking out. An eight-piece orchestra played “Pachelbel’s Canon” over and over.

The adults decided not to wear out the flower girl, so only when the rest of the bridal party was sure of their parts did the director turn to Danika. “Okay, little lady. It’s time for you to walk in front of the bride.”

The plan was for Kellan and Vaughn to flank their sister on either side going down the aisle. But already Danika was showing signs of being overwhelmed by the setting and all the strangers.

Brie and Sophie both talked to her, but it was Vaughn who saved the day. He squatted in front of his daughter and spoke to her at eye level with a gentle smile. “Here’s what I’ll do, Nika.” He pointed toward the length of the ivory satin runner. “I’ll sit on the end of that aisle way up there and you can walk to me. How about that? And you can drop the flowers while you’re coming to meet me.”

Something in the tone of his voice or in his words reassured the not-quite two-year-old. Brie’s heart melted at the interaction between father and child. She didn’t know Vaughn had it in him.

Sophie and Kellan quickly moved into position. Vaughn loped to the front of the tent. The director gave a wave to the orchestra, who started playing once again.

Brie handed Danika her basket and gave her a little nudge. “Go to Mr. V. He’s waiting for you.”

As Brie watched, fingers crossed, Nika started walking and tossing flower petals as if she had been doing it her entire life. Sophie began to cry sentimental tears. Kellan gave her a handkerchief.

It took a while. But the bride was in no hurry.

Eventually, the woman of the hour and her hesitant petal tosser made it into position in front of the minister. Everyone breathed a collective sigh of relief.

After a quick conference with the bride, the director deemed the rehearsal satisfactory.

Vaughn hoisted Nika on his shoulders and came back to where Brie was standing. "How did it look from back here?"

"Perfect. Charming. Now, if she'll only do it tomorrow."

Vaughn grinned. "I have faith in her."

Brie lifted Danika down from her perch and took her daughter's hand. "I've got her dinner in the car. As soon as I feed her, I have a friend who is going to swap cars with me and take her home so I can stay for the rest of the evening."

Vaughn frowned. "A friend?"

"A college student home on spring break, actually. I've known her and her parents for a long time. Tabitha will put Nika to bed and stay with her until I get home."

"How do we know she's trustworthy?"

It was Brie's turn to smile. "Good grief, Vaughn. I'm not sending my only child home with a stranger. Tabitha knows Nika and me. And I know her. She's as good as it gets when it comes to babysitters. Nika will be fine."

Seventeen

Vaughn didn't like it, but he could see the sense in Brie's plan. There was no way a two-year-old could make it through a long, fancy dinner. Instead, Danika was soon settled, eating a cheese sandwich, enjoying the novelty of being perched in the back of the car and, at the same time, ignoring the adults.

"Okay. If you've got this covered, I'm going to go back in and talk to Sophie. Apparently my big-hearted sister has invited the stepwitch to the rehearsal dinner, God knows why."

Brie stared at him oddly. "Well, Blackwood Hollow *is* Miranda's home now. And she's been kind enough to let Sophie have her wedding here. I really don't see what you have against Miranda, Vaughn. It's not her fault that your father made that crazy will."

"Doesn't mean I have to like her." His chest tightened, thinking about the injustice of it all.

Brie leaned against the car, hands propped behind her. She studied his face. "Is it so terribly hard to be back here at Blackwood Hollow?"

He thought about it. So far today, he'd been running on adrenaline. Now he gave the question serious consideration. "Yes and no," he said slowly. "This is the first time since the will reading for me. I don't know about the others. There are plenty of bad memories here—but there are good ones, too. I like remembering Mom when she wasn't sick. When she was happy and productive and all of us kids were running around. Those were good days."

"Isn't that why Sophie wanted the wedding here? To remember your past and honor your mom?"

"Yes."

"So maybe Sophie is grateful to Miranda for making that possible."

"I suppose." He glanced over his shoulder at the tents and made a snap decision. "If Miranda is here, I don't want to miss our chance to establish Danika's claim to the inheritance." He reached in his pocket. "Here. Put this on."

Brie's expression was not what he had anticipated. She seemed both shocked and horrified, if that were possible.

"This was one of my mother's rings," he said. "We want this engagement to look like the real deal." Since Brie was making no move to take the heavy piece of jewelry, he slid it onto her finger. "I want you to keep it when this is all over. The stone will look good with your eyes." Donna-Leigh Blackwood had been a stunner in her day. The engagement ring was a huge, perfectly rectangular aquamarine surrounded by a rim of sparkling diamonds.

Brie seemed *stricken*, or something. He couldn't read her. "I can't keep this," she said. "It's far too valuable, not to mention impractical for a vet to wear to work."

"It will be Danika's someday. Wear it. Don't wear it. But tonight, it's important." He glanced at his watch. "I've got to get back over there and see what's going on."

Brie nodded, her expression unreadable. "I'll text you when I'm heading back inside."

Vaughn strode away from the two females, feeling out of sorts. In his heart, he had thought Brie would be happy to wear his mother's ring, even if for only a short while. Instead, he had the distinct impression he had insulted her.

Women. No wonder he had stayed away from entanglements all these years. They were too much trouble.

When he rejoined the bridal group, everyone had moved from the tent where the ceremony was to take place into the second tent that had been set up for a lavish dinner of prime rib and all the accoutrements. The spread looked amazing. But no one seemed to be in charge of crowd control.

The Brits were obviously flagging. They hadn't been here long enough yet to be over their jet lag, and it was late back in England. By contrast, all the bridesmaids and groomsmen were laughing and talking and enjoying the open bar.

Vaughn found Sophie, Nigel and Kellan. "I think everyone is hungry. Why don't we get them seated so the servers can begin?"

Nigel nodded. "Indeed." He put his fingers to his lips and gave a loud, perfect whistle.

The crowd stilled instantly. Nigel waved a hand. "Find your place cards, ladies and gentlemen. The meal is about to begin. Thank you for joining us this evening."

With that taken care of, Vaughn took Sophie's hand. "Is Miranda really here?"

Sophie's gaze narrowed. "You will *not* cause a scene, Vaughn Blackwood. This is my wedding weekend."

"Not to worry. I'll be good as gold. I just need to tell her something."

Sophie pursed her lips. "And you might as well know, Kace is with her."

"Kace?" Vaughn scowled. "Why? Isn't he newly engaged to that Lulu person?"

Nigel intervened. "Come on, old chap. Lighten up. This is a party. No one is going to upset my angel."

"Sorry," Vaughn muttered.

In that instant, Brie appeared. As she approached from a distance, Vaughn's heart kicked in his chest. He'd been so focused on his master plan and Miranda, he hadn't stopped to appreciate how damned beautiful Brie looked.

She had worn her hair down tonight, masses of golden waves that framed her face and made her look both appealing and vulnerable. The gown she wore was dressy but perfect for an outdoor event—a frothy confection of royal blue and silver tulle over satin. The bodice was fitted at the waist, where the dress fanned out in a full skirt that stopped just above her knees. When he glanced at her hand, he saw that she hadn't removed the ring.

The jolt of pleasure he got from seeing the ring on her finger was concerning. Why should he care that his mark of possession was on her hand? It wasn't as if any of this was real.

A tiny voice inside his head told him it *could* be. Real, that was. Real and permanent and life changing.

It was that last bit that worried him the most. He liked his life. Didn't he? Why tinker with something that had been working extremely well? This deal with McCready was a perfect example of why Vaughn was so successful. He knew how to negotiate and when to step back.

He was a damned good businessman.

Three steps in her direction, and he could take her hand. "I didn't say it before, but you look amazing tonight."

Her smile was shy. "Thanks. We were both busy earlier. I can relax now that Danika's part is over."

"Indeed. Shall we go find our seats?" He tucked her hand in the crook of his arm.

Before they could follow Sophie and Nigel and Kellan, Vaughn saw Miranda Blackwood and Kace LeBlanc appear. Along with Darius Taylor-Pratt and

Audra. Vaughn recognized Darius and Audra from pictures Sophie had sent him.

Vaughn's stomach tightened, but he gave his new sibling a curt nod in response to Miranda's introductions.

"Hello." Darius reciprocated with a subdued greeting.

The expression on Kace's face stopped them all in their tracks. "I know this is a special occasion, but Miranda has some very important news. Kellan, you'll need to get Irina. Sophie. Nigel. Vaughn. Let's step into the other tent, since it's empty now. Darius, you and Audra, too."

Vaughn bristled. "Slow down a minute. If this is family business, then Brie should be there. You should all know—Brie and I are engaged." He held up her hand to show off the ring. "And Danika is our daughter."

After a moment of pregnant silence, Miranda spoke, smiling wryly. "I'm happy for you. And of course, Brie should join us, as well."

Moments later, the ten adults stood inside the tent where Sophie and Nigel would become husband and wife tomorrow.

Kace LeBlanc, Miranda's lawyer, was less brusque than normal. If anything, his quiet words were conciliatory.

"Miranda has asked me to share some news with you. When your father died, he left a convoluted will, as you know. The truth is, Buckley made Miranda the temporary caretaker of his estate—not his true heir. He died old and alone because of a series of bad choices he made, particularly in the realm of relationships. He was most insistent that the same fate not befall each of you. Miranda was charged with protecting and running the estate until such time as Buckley's three children—Kellan, Sophie and Vaughn—showed evidence of personal growth, maturity and the ability to connect meaningfully with another human being. I'm quoting, by the way."

Miranda nodded. "My instructions came in the form of three letters. The initial set of demands was in the first letter, just as Kace has explained."

"And the second?" Vaughn asked sharply.

Miranda gave him a level stare. "The second letter involved finding Darius and legitimizing his claim to the estate."

"Which Darius knew nothing about," Kace reminded them.

Sophie was pale. "And the third letter?"

"It will be revealed in good time," Miranda said. "But you should know that it's the least significant of the three. The contents of the last letter won't impact anyone in a significant way. It's my instructions from the first one that I'm ready to put into action now." She grimaced. "I know what you all thought of me when it looked like I'd gotten all of your father's estate, but I didn't *want* anything of Buckley's. I still don't. Kace and I have determined that by every benchmark, you each have met Buckley's requirements. Vaughn, I didn't know you were engaged, but you have certainly made a point of being supportive of Kellan and Sophie during these difficult months."

Kace picked up the story again. "Kellan, the ranch is yours, free and clear."

Kellan blinked and muttered a shocked curse. "What about the others?"

Kace continued. "Blackwood Bank and all its assets go to Vaughn. Sophie, you inherit several houses and a large sum of cash. You can let me know how you want the payout, since it will affect your tax status."

"And Darius?" Sophie asked.

Miranda smiled. "He's to receive a lump sum of cash as well, which I'm guessing he'll invest in his business."

Darius nodded, looking stunned.

Kace sighed. "That's the gist of it. Any questions?"

No one moved at first. Then Sophie stepped forward and shook Miranda's hand briefly. "Thank you for doing this impossible job. And thank you for allowing Nigel and me to get married at Blackwood Hollow in spite of the way I treated you after the will reading. That was very generous of you, under the circumstances. I hope we can all eventually be friends."

Kellan chuckled. "Or at least not enemies."

Irina punched him in the arm.

Vaughn didn't know what to think. His head was spinning. "We should get back to the party," he said, keeping his tone cool, hoping to let Miranda know that he didn't forgive as easily as *some* people in his family.

Nigel nodded. "Vaughn is right. Kace and Miranda, you are invited guests, as Sophie has told you. I hope you'll stay and help us celebrate. This weekend is a time for looking to the future."

Moments later, Vaughn and Brie were the only two lingering in the tent. "Are you okay?" she asked quietly. "I thought you would be happy and excited. And as it turns out, our little fictional engagement was not even necessary."

He shook his head slowly. "I'm not sure I know *what* I feel. I never liked being manipulated by my father in real life. Having him do it from the grave is almost as demeaning."

Brie shook her head disbelievingly. "You're the only person I know who can inherit a fortune and still be miffed about it."

"I'm not miffed," he said, "but I don't appreciate having to prove my worth."

"In all fairness, Miranda and Kace were handing over the bank to you even before you told them you and I are engaged. So I'd say they definitely gave you the benefit of the doubt."

"I suppose so."

"Let's go eat," Brie said. "I'm starving."

"Okay. But afterward, I'd like to drive around the ranch and visit old haunts."

Brie's eyes widened. "You mean like haylofts?"

He lifted one shoulder and let it fall, feigning innocence. "Whatever takes our fancy."

For the next hour, Vaughn talked and ate and gave a winning performance of the man without a care in the world. He and Kellan both toasted the bride and groom.

But old words came back to haunt him. *You're probably the most like me.*

Was it true? The question made his stomach queasy. On bad days, he had hated his father at times. Even on good days, he'd disdained him. How would Danika look at Vaughn one day?

The uncomfortable question tormented him.

And what about Brie? She was seated beside him, of course. But somehow he sensed a distance between them that hadn't been there before.

Kellan and Irina were on the opposite side of the table. At one point, late in the evening, Kellan yawned and leaned back in his chair. "It's been great having you in Royal for so long, Vaughn. When do you have to go home?"

"I'm flying out tomorrow evening…after the wedding. Business calls," he said lightly.

Eighteen

Brie sat stunned, trying to control her facial expressions. Vaughn was leaving town tomorrow? This was the first she had heard of it. The fact that he hadn't thought to mention it told her more loudly than words that Vaughn Blackwood hadn't changed a bit.

He had a cash register—a calculator—where his heart should be. Sure, he might have warmed up to Danika, but he had no plans to alter his life in any meaningful way, no intent to include Brie and her daughter in his sterile, business-centered sphere.

The hurt ran deep. Anger, too. She was angry at herself for weaving dreams that had no basis in reality. What a fool she was. Not only had she blinded herself to Vaughn's true nature, but she had fallen in love with him again.

Perhaps that last part wasn't quite true. Maybe she had never *quit* loving him. Maybe she had been in denial for almost three years. Pregnant and alone. Giving birth. Rearing a baby with little emotional or financial support.

And all along, deep down inside, she had held out hope for the future. Wasn't that ultimately why she had moved back to Royal? To be near his family and thus be sure she and Vaughn would eventually cross paths again?

The depths of her own self-deception were stunning.

Even recently, she'd pretended that she knew Vaughn was the proverbial rolling stone…that she had to end their physical relationship because he would be leaving.

But somewhere deep in her vulnerable woman's heart, she had thought she could change him.

Her skin felt cold and clammy. The meal she had consumed rolled in her stomach. She wanted to go home to her baby, to the one person who loved her unconditionally.

Abruptly, she stood and made her way to Sophie and Nigel's table. "I need to head out," she said, feigning cheerfulness. "Danika will be up very early, and I want to make sure our day gets off to a good start in the morning, so she'll be fresh for the wedding."

Sophie and Nigel stood to hug her and extend their thanks. Then Brie turned and fled, only to run into the solid bulk of her faux fiancé. "What are you doing?" he asked, frowning. Did the man ever do anything *but* frown?

She couldn't meet his eyes. She kept walking quickly

toward the tent exit, forcing him to follow. "I have to relieve Tabitha so she can go home."

Outside, he took her arm. "You told me she was prepared to stay until midnight. It's only ten o'clock. What's your rush, Brie?"

Tears burned her eyelids. She blinked them back, determined not to reveal her weakness, her incredibly hopeless yearning.

She sucked in a deep breath of the air that was far cooler here than that in the tent and exhaled slowly. "I'm tired," she said simply. "Today was a long day, and tomorrow will be the same. Good night, Vaughn."

He shackled her wrist with one big hand and drew her close. "You're upset. I know you that well. Tell me what's wrong. Did I do something?"

It was impossible to answer without incriminating herself. "No," she lied. "It's not you."

He stroked her hair, gentling her as he would a spooked filly. Brie knew the drill. She had done the same thing a hundred times on this very ranch.

His voice was low and rough when he spoke. "You wanted to know how I felt about being back here. I should ask you the same question. Is that what's bothering you, Brie? Does being here bring back too many memories?"

Gradually, she let the cool night air and Vaughn's steady touch settle her. "Yes," she said simply. "Being here reminds me of all my mistakes. I was young and not ambitious enough. I knew I wanted my own vet practice, but I let Buckley take advantage of me."

"Why?"

She shrugged. "Because I loved the ranch and the horses..." *And you.*

He was silent for a moment. "Will you get in the car with me? I won't keep you long. We both need some closure. Perhaps exorcising a few ghosts will help you sleep tonight."

Brie knew he wasn't talking about their relationship. But on a deeper level, she could hear his question in those terms. Vaughn was flying home tomorrow. Tonight would be her last chance to make love to him.

Was that what she wanted?

"Okay," she said, feeling the noose of inevitability tighten around her throat. "Sure. Let's drive."

Vaughn's car was parked nearby. He helped her in and shut the door, careful not to catch her skirt.

The night was perfect for a convertible. He put the top down so they could enjoy the stars. Gravel crunched beneath the tires. In the distance, the ranch house loomed. Not a single light shone. With Buckley dead and Miranda at the party, there was no one left to walk the halls.

Vaughn passed the house and drove on to the collection of barns and outbuildings where Brie had worked so many long, hard hours. Despite the drawbacks, it had been good experience for her. She knew that now. But letting the old man's son seduce her had been a mistake.

Still, Brie had gotten her beloved Danika out of the bargain, so even that long-ago mistake wasn't so bad in retrospect.

The convertible rolled to a halt in the shadow of the largest and fanciest of the barns, the one with an entire double row of stalls. The one where Brie had honed her talents and enthusiasm for horses into the skills that made her such a good vet. She loved their beauty and spirit, loved keeping them healthy and productive.

Both adults got out of the car. Far in the distance, Brie could hear that the music had started for dancing. Not the orchestra anymore, but a rowdy country band. Who knew how Nigel's family would take to that? Perhaps his grandmother would learn how to line dance.

Vaughn strode toward the barn, not waiting to see if Brie was following. When he hauled back the heavy wooden door and turned on a track of diffused light, a host of smells and sounds wafted out. Simple. Familiar. Evocative.

Hay and feed. Old wood and new leather. The soft whicker of a mare. The deeper snorting of an alpha stallion.

It was like stepping back in time.

Until this very moment, Brie honestly hadn't realized how much she missed this place. Buckley might have been a difficult man, but he had built an impressive empire. He'd also helped raise three adult children who were each outstanding in their own right.

Vaughn had walked on ahead, stopping under the center pitch of the roof. As he looked up, Brie saw him in profile. His shoulders stretched the tailored seams of his charcoal-gray suit. His features were classic, masculine.

No broken nose or shaggy haircut to mar his physical perfection and make him seem more human. Everything about him was crisp and professional and...unreachable.

Maybe Vaughn didn't need a woman in his life at all.

She closed the gap between them, assailed by memories that wrapped around her heart and squeezed. There were no more poignant words in the English language than *if only...*

Leaning her head against his shoulder, she gave herself permission to let him go. Vaughn represented a time in her life when she was footloose and free. Nothing to tie her down but the need for a paycheck.

Brie was a different woman now. Motherhood had changed her priorities. Unfortunately, the only part of her that remained the same was the hunger for Vaughn's touch.

He slid an arm around her waist, his gaze still fixed on the high point of the vaulted ceiling with the open rafters. "I walked the roofline of this barn once," he said. "Did I ever tell you that?" He pointed over his head. "Had to shimmy out that small window right there and drag myself on up to the top."

"No. You never told me. Sounds dangerous."

"Oh yeah," he chuckled. "It was. I was fifteen and dumb as a bag of rocks. My father had made me angry about something, and in my convoluted adolescent brain, I decided that literally looking down on him and his stupid ranch would give me the advantage."

"Did it?"

He rubbed the back of his neck with his free hand and gave her a rueful grin. "Not that I can remember. What I *do* remember is sitting up there for more than three hours, because I couldn't figure out how to get down without killing myself."

"What did your father do?"

"Not a damn thing. He never knew. Actually, he took the truck into town that afternoon. While he was gone, Sophie and Kellan got an extension ladder to help rescue me. Soph cried the entire time. I felt like a jackass."

"Are you jealous that Kellan inherited Blackwood Hollow and not you?"

He hesitated. "It gave me a twinge to hear it wouldn't be mine," he admitted. "But Kellan deserves it. Besides, my life is in Fort Worth. What would I do with the ranch other than get someone else to run it for me? It's all for the best."

"I suppose."

He turned her to face him and kissed her softly. "What do you say, Brie? Are you up for climbing the ladder?"

The hayloft didn't run the length of the barn. It barely covered one corner. The majority of the ranch's hay was stored in a separate facility, but a couple dozen bales were kept nearby for convenience's sake.

Vaughn and Brie had found them very convenient indeed.

She kicked off her shoes. "I am."

His gaze flared with heat. She saw the muscles in his throat ripple.

While he shrugged out of his jacket and loosened his tie, she told herself she needed one last walk on the wild side before she settled down to be a typical middle-class mom with bills and a kid in school and dreams of what might have been.

The truth was even simpler. She loved Vaughn and didn't want to say goodbye.

He pulled her toward the ladder. "You first," he said. "I'll catch you if you fall."

She put one bare foot on the bottom rung and quickly scooted up the ladder, feeling self-conscious about her bare legs and other parts. Vaughn was right behind her. He had more upper-body strength and was taller, so he wasn't breathing hard at all when they stepped out onto the solid platform.

Nothing much had changed. Even the old, faded quilt was still there, shoved over in a corner.

Brie wrinkled her nose. "I'm not sitting down on that."

Vaughn laughed, looking remarkably carefree for once. "I'll be the one sitting. Wouldn't want to damage that beautiful dress." He caught her wrist and reeled her in. "Kiss me, Brie."

The mood shifted in a heartbeat. Up to this point, they both had been dealing with nostalgia and perhaps regret. Now, deeper emotions surfaced.

His lips were firm and warm and coaxing, as if he knew she was conflicted. Strong arms encircled her waist. Big hands cupped her bottom and lifted her against his chest.

She felt dizzy and breathless. His skin smelled warm and male. It seemed like they were the only people in the world. No one knew they were here. Everyone else was occupied.

Her heart thumped in her chest. She wound her legs around his hips, nipping his chin with a sharp, quick nibble. “I could never say no to you,” she complained. “You dazzled me.”

“Wrong.” His quick frown was dark. “*You* were the one who bewitched me, Brie. I came home one weekend to conduct some necessary business with my father. The next thing I knew, I was commuting back and forth twice a week, trying not to let anyone know why I was suddenly so enamored with being back in Royal. I panted after you like a puppy dog, but you were maddeningly hard to read. I used to wish you came with a manual so I could figure out what the hell you wanted.”

His sudden burst of frustration shocked her. “I wasn’t playing games, Vaughn. I was just happy to be with you.”

“But it wasn’t enough, was it?”

She couldn’t answer that. They both knew the truth. Brie had wanted and needed promises. Security.

Vaughn had been unable to deliver any of that and unwilling to pretend he could be that kind of man. So their relationship had unraveled, and Brie had moved away.

With a sigh, she rested her forehead against his. “Life is always about timing. You and I had something wonderful back then. Let’s not ruin the memories by arguing. I want to be with you tonight. But I have to go home soon.”

His muffled grunt wasn’t an answer. He carried her to the nearest, newest-looking bale of hay and sat down with her in his lap. His hands settled on her waist. “You outshone the bride tonight, Brie. Even if she is my sister.”

“Thank you.” What would happen if she told him

she loved him? If she begged him to give up his life in Dallas/Fort Worth and stay in Royal with her?

To be fair, she would have to think long and hard if he turned the tables. Could she abandon her brand-new, thriving practice and move to Forth Worth? For a man with no track record in regard to long-term commitment?

The urge to blurt out three words was strong. *I love you.* If Brie had been on her own, the only risk would be heartbreak. But Danika was a factor in this equation. Even now, Brie couldn't tell if Vaughn wanted to be a father or not.

She sifted her fingers through his thick, healthy hair. "I hope you came prepared."

His chuckle sounded hoarse and breathless. "You can bet on it, Brie."

She sucked in a sharp breath when his thumbs caressed the insides of her thighs, making her legs quiver. The subtle torture sent her higher. Wiggling so he would get the idea, she mentally urged him closer. Needy and urgent, she wanted it all.

Her breasts ached for his touch, for his possession. "Please," she croaked, shaking.

At last, he moved. He fumbled in his pants for the condom and applied it quickly. Then he gave her a smile that was both sweet and searing hot. Her undies ended up on the floor with Houdini-like speed.

"I've been waiting for this all day," he said, the words barely audible. With one hard push, he was inside her, huge and hard and crazy wonderful.

Her body tightened instinctively around him. "Yes," she whispered, her eyes squeezed shut. "Yes."

Something told her this would be the last time. Grief and joy mingled, odd bedfellows indeed. Vaughn's big, warm hands kneaded her ass, his labored breath warm on her neck as he buried his face in her shoulder.

"Brie," he muttered. "Brie."

She could almost tell herself he loved her. But he had never said the words, and she had come too far to believe in fantasy now.

Instead of wishing for the moon, she closed her eyes and gave in to the moment. It was enough. It had to be.

Nineteen

In the midst of sheer, physical bliss, Brie found herself sad…resigned. Vaughn held her close against his heaving chest—not saying much at first. "We have to talk about a few things before I leave town tomorrow," he said eventually.

Brie stiffened. "It's going to be a busy day."

"I know. But this is important."

Brie stood and reached for her missing item of clothing. "I have to get back to Danika," she said quietly. "I'm sorry to rush away."

"I understand. Why don't I drive you? I can get someone else to follow us with the babysitter's car."

His expression was impossible to read in the dim light. "Thank you, but no," she said. "Sophie is your only sister. You've already skipped out on the party for too long. Go back. Play your part. Nika and I will see you at the wedding in the morning."

After that, the silence grew. Their lovemaking had been off-the-charts good by any standard. Brie cried out his name when she came. But they might as well have been miles apart.

As she descended the ladder with him right below her, she swallowed her dismay. At the bottom, she found her shoes and rummaged for a small towel to wipe her feet.

Vaughn wanted to do it for her. She stepped away and handled it herself.

Then she walked out of the barn to the car. She was waiting for him in the passenger seat after he turned off the lights and closed the big door.

Not a word was spoken during the brief drive back to the sitter's parked car. Danika and Tabitha had taken Brie's vehicle with the car seat.

Brie fished keys out of her evening purse. "Good night, Vaughn."

He took her wrist. Gently. No coercion. "We'll figure this out. Danika deserves the best of both of us."

"I know."

This time, he kissed her forehead. The international symbol for *I think we should just be friends.* "Be careful going home."

"I will."

When she couldn't bear the awkward tension between them any longer, she stepped back and seated herself in the unfamiliar car. Vaughn was little more than a shadow in the darkness.

Brie reversed, pulled out and drove away.

* * *

Danika woke up all smiles the following morning. The evening with the sitter had been a novelty, and Tabitha had reported it went very well.

Brie was far less perky than her daughter.

Three cups of coffee and she was still not herself. It hadn't been smart to lie awake for hours thinking about Vaughn. Not smart at all. Now, not only was she facing a stressful day, but she was going into it with an exhaustion hangover.

They made it out to Blackwood Hollow right on time. Some of the pictures were being taken beforehand, including the ones with Sophie, all her bridesmaids and Danika.

Brie was relieved that her daughter cooperated. The ceremony itself would come and go, but pictures lasted forever.

A light breeze kept the temperature in the tent comfortable. Sophie seemed in good spirits, laughing and beaming. The men were sequestered in the other tent where the rehearsal dinner had taken place the night before.

Vaughn being absent was a good thing. Brie didn't know what to say to him. She was all out of words.

Brie still thought Vaughn should be at his sister's side going down the aisle, but the siblings had discussed it and decided it was more important for Vaughn to coax his daughter to the front.

Suddenly, without warning, it was time.

Brie had witnessed the influx of guests, hundreds of them, laughing and chatting excitedly as the crowd swelled. Most fit into the space for the ceremony, but perhaps three dozen latecomers were tucked away in the rear tent watching on a video feed.

The groomsmen and bridesmaids lined up two by two. Then Danika, then the bride.

The prelude music began.

Tears filled Brie's eyes. She was happy for Sophie.

As the attendants played their parts, moving with measured steps along the satin runner, Kellan and Sophie exchanged a hug. Two siblings out of three happily married. Those were good odds.

The wedding director gave Brie a harried smile. "Time for the flower girl."

Brie crouched and tucked a curl behind Nika's ear. "Walk to Mr. V," she said, her throat tight. "Just like you did last night."

Danika beamed and stepped out, suddenly ready to perform. Her dress was perfect, her sweet smile adorable. The crowd loved it and responded audibly.

Brie met Vaughn's gaze over the long distance that separated them. He gave Brie a thumbs-up, or perhaps the gesture was for the two-year-old.

Then Sophie and Kellan took their places. The music swelled. The crowd stood. The bride walked down the aisle.

During the brief but meaningful ceremony, Brie stood at the back of the tent, feeling a bit lost. Danika was safe and happy with her father. Brie was superfluous at the moment.

Was this how it would be if she and Vaughn shared

custody? Would Brie spend half her days feeling oddly at loose ends whenever it was Vaughn's turn to have Nika?

For one selfish moment, she hoped he would bow out completely. It would be so much easier to rear Danika on her own. And Brie wouldn't have to see Vaughn over and over again.

But even as the thought flitted through her mind, she knew it was wrong. Nika needed her daddy, and though he might not realize it, Vaughn needed his daughter.

It was Kellan's wife, Irina, who took Danika's hand after the ceremony and walked the little girl back to Brie. Vaughn had disappeared with Kellan.

Brie thanked Vaughn's sister-in-law. "What's up with the guys? Where did they run off to? Don't they know this is a special occasion?"

Irina rolled her eyes. "Something about an important business deal in Dallas. Now that Kellan for sure has the ranch, he wants to invest in Vaughn's company."

"Ah."

The two women exchanged wry glances. Irina shook her head. "I've learned you can't tame a Texan. We're the ones who have to change and adapt."

"But you look radiant and happy."

Irina grinned. "Oh, I am. Kellan is the love of my life. He may be stubborn, but he dotes on me."

After the woman walked away, Brie stayed put for a minute, pondering Irina's words. Was Brie willing to make compromises for a shot at happiness? She honestly didn't know. How much was too much to bend?

Unlike last night, the reception was not nearby. All

the guests had to load up and head across town to the posh Bellamy resort, where the wedding brunch was to be held.

The bride and groom had arranged for fully staffed babysitting—by reservation—at the TCC childcare center. The new Mr. and Mrs. Townshend had even catered munchkin-friendly food for the little ones' meals. Having the option was a relief. A formal wedding brunch at the elegant Bellamy was definitely not the place for kids.

Brie dropped Danika off at the center on the way. Nika was comfortable there by now and went without protest.

At the Bellamy, the scene was organized chaos. A larger-than-normal staff of valets was parking cars. Brie handed over her keys and tucked the claim ticket in her small beaded purse.

On one side of the entrance, Nigel's unmistakably upper-crust family gathered as they were dropped off. Coincidentally, the opposite portion of the driveway had been overtaken with the cast and crew of the *Secret Lives* show.

Nigel and Sophie had invited all the wives and even granted camera access to the reception, within reason. Brie spotted Miranda entering the hotel alone. Something about Miranda's dignified posture made Brie feel sorry for her. Miranda had done her best in a difficult situation.

As Brie made her way to the salon where the brunch was being served, a warm male hand descended on her shoulder. "There you are," said a familiar voice.

She felt her cheeks go hot. "Hello, Vaughn."

He cocked his head, his lips twitching. "That's all you've got to say after last night?"

"I have no idea to what you are referring," she said primly.

She was wearing an ankle-length gown spangled with tiny, tiny bugle beads. The halter neck left her shoulders bare.

Vaughn traced her collarbone with a fingertip, his gaze hooded. "This tangerine color suits you. I have a few ideas for getting you undressed later."

Her spine stiffened. "You're flying out later. Remember?" Perhaps he heard the tart bite in her voice.

"Details, details." He took her elbow. "Come on. I found our seats already. And for the record, I'm starving."

The long, gorgeous room had been decked out as a conservatory. Lush plants, everything from hibiscus to orchids, lined the corridors and graced the tables. Nigel and Sophie's table was slightly raised, so the bride and groom could see all their guests.

Champagne flowed like water. Waiters with trays of mimosas in Baccarat crystal flutes circulated among the crowd.

At last everyone was seated, and the meal began. After the main course of raspberry crepes, eggs Benedict and honeyed dates, Nigel's grandmother stood and regaled the group with rather saucy tales of his childhood. Brie smiled inwardly at seeing the proper Englishman be mortified by his own granny.

Vaughn and Kellan had their own set of stories about

Sophie. The bride pretended to be insulted, but Brie could see that she loved the attention from the brothers she adored.

Then it was time for dessert. Someone from the kitchen wheeled out an enormous cart laden with the most beautiful wedding cake Brie had even seen. It was covered in pastel-pink-and-white fondant and adorned with tiny, handmade sugar ribbons and roses.

After Sophie and Nigel cut the cake, feeding each other in the process, the kitchen crew quickly sliced and served the masterpiece to every guest…with more alcohol for those who wanted it.

Vaughn whispered in her ear, "You have icing on the side of your mouth," he said softly, leaning forward and removing it with his thumb. Then he sucked his thumb and smiled. "Delicious."

Beneath the pristine linen tablecloth, Brie pressed her knees together. The man was a devil. "Stop that," she hissed. "People are watching us."

It was true. Nigel's large family and Sophie's smaller one, including Dixie Musgraves, were seated on either end of the dais, facing the rest of the guests. It was impossible to adjust a bra strap or remove food from your teeth without someone noticing.

After the cake cutting, there was a brief lull. Sophie and Nigel had exited for a brief moment alone, promising to return shortly for the obligatory bouquet toss.

Brie needed a breath of air. Though she had only consumed a single mimosa, her head was spinning. "I'm going to visit the ladies' room," she said. "Be right back."

The lobby of the hotel was oddly silent. Most of the resort's rooms had been overtaken by out-of-town wedding guests, so the most likely explanation was that everyone involved was occupied with brunch.

Just as Brie was crossing the wide expanse of lush carpet, a man intersected her path. He was a couple of decades her senior. His longish, dark blond hair wasn't her preference, but he still possessed an attractive boyish charm.

It took Brie a moment to recognize him as Vaughn's lawyer. Her stomach clenched. "Mr. Matthews. I didn't expect to see you today." He was dressed in a worn tux.

"Ms. Sophie is kind to an old guy like me. I appreciated the invitation."

Brie manufactured a smile. "If you'll excuse me…"

She turned to pursue her original errand, but the lawyer halted her with a hand on her arm. She shook off his touch. "I'm in a hurry," she said curtly, no longer willing to feign social niceties now that she remembered who he was.

"Wait," he insisted, touching her a second time. "I have something for you." He pulled a standard-size manila envelope from his inside breast pocket. It was folded in half lengthwise. "Vaughn wanted me to give you these."

Brie felt a chill on her skin. A premonition. Automatically, she took the envelope and flattened it where it had been folded. Almost without thinking, she withdrew the stack of pages. Not that many. Ten, maybe. Twelve at the most.

“What is this?” she asked, nausea rippling through her stomach as she took in words and phrases.

“Just a standard business thing,” Trent said breezily. “Mr. McCready and your fiancé have to protect the integrity of their very important deal. All we’re doing is asking you to sign this and verify that you and the kid aren’t going to make any kind of claims on the profits. Which is only fair,” he said quickly, “since this acquisition was underway before the two of you came on the scene.”

“My daughter’s name is Danika,” Brie said carefully.

Her heart lay in ashes at her feet. She had anticipated getting hurt because she was more invested in this relationship than Vaughn. What she had never seen coming was such careless cruelty. She’d hoped Vaughn had changed…that his relationship with her and with Nika had become more important to him than profit or a bottom line.

Even in the midst of her distress, she paused, unwilling to convict her faux fiancé unfairly. She stared Trent Matthews straight in the eyes. “Has Vaughn Blackwood seen these papers?”

Matthews never hesitated. His head cocked to one side, a mildly puzzled smile on his face. “Of course.”

Twenty

Vaughn checked his watch for the third time. Brie had been gone twenty-five minutes. He assumed she would call the TCC to check on Danika, but even so, she should have been back by now.

Absently, he noticed that Trent Matthews was standing on the opposite side of the room near a doorway. The man's expression was equal parts affable and satisfied. Why had Sophie invited him?

And then it dawned on Vaughn—she probably hadn't. Trent Matthews was exactly the kind of man who would crash a wedding. Something wasn't right.

Just when Vaughn was ready to go in search of Brie, she appeared, sliding into her seat with an apologetic smile.

"Everything okay?" he whispered. She was pale, and her forehead was damp.

"Yes," she said, reaching for her water glass. "Shh. Nigel is about to say something."

The bride and groom were inviting everyone into the adjoining ballroom for dancing and more festivities. The crowd rose as one, eager to continue the party.

In the commotion, Brie slipped something into his pocket. "When I called the TCC center, they said Danika has been asking for me. I'm going to take her home for a nap."

Vaughn frowned. "I'll go with you."

"No, no," Brie said. Her gaze didn't quite meet his. "You have to be here for your family. It's a big day for the Blackwoods."

She went up on tiptoe and kissed him on the cheek. "Tell Sophie that Danika loved her gig. Goodbye, Vaughn."

People jostled on both sides. He reached for Brie's arm, but she eluded him, getting lost in the crowd.

Vaughn cursed. But he was trapped. He and Kellan were both supposed to dance with the bride in a moment, during what was usually the father/daughter dance. Brie was right. He couldn't go.

In the ballroom, the crowd thinned out, lining both sides of the dance floor. Sophie and Nigel had the first dance, of course. Then it was Kellan's turn. Vaughn wanted to see what Brie had tucked in his pocket, but he was in a visible position and had to play his part.

When Vaughn took Sophie in his arms, his immediate frustration eased. "Have I told you how gorgeous you look, Soph? It was a great day."

She rested her head on his shoulder, smothering a

yawn. “And it’s not over yet. Nigel and I have to finish packing a few last-minute items. Our flight to Europe leaves tonight at six.”

“And the Townshend entourage?”

“They’ll all be heading out in the morning.” Sophie leaned back and studied his face. “Are you okay, Vaughn?”

“Of course,” he said automatically.

“Are you and Brie…” She trailed off, clearly unwilling to press him.

“I don’t know what Brie and I are,” he admitted.

“You’re my brother. I want you to be happy.”

He kissed her forehead. “I’m as happy as I deserve. Don’t worry about me, sis. I always land on my feet.”

The song ended, and a chunk of the guests surged onto the floor, eager to join the fun.

For Vaughn, this was his cue to cut out. Unobtrusively, he made his way toward the exit, pausing now and then for quick conversations when he couldn’t completely elude someone.

At last, he made it out into a quiet corridor.

When he pulled an envelope from his pocket, his heart stopped. It was a piece of hotel stationery. The seal had barely held because of something bulky inside.

He ripped it open, catching the aquamarine and diamond ring that tumbled out. He wasn’t entirely surprised. Brie had never wanted to keep it from the beginning.

With shaking hands, he unfolded the single piece of paper inside.

Dear Vaughn,
I hope you have a safe and pleasant return flight to Dallas/Fort Worth. Once your life is back to normal, please give some thought to the Danika situation. I won't judge you, whatever you decide. Your choice has to come from the heart. If you feel unwilling or unable to play a role as her father, I understand.

I'm returning the ring. Please tuck it away in a safe somewhere. Perhaps you'll want to give it to Nika one day.

I have signed the McCready papers and left them at the front desk. But I didn't want to take a chance with something as valuable as the ring.
Wishing you all the best,
Brie

Vaughn was in shock. This was a goodbye note, plain and simple. Brie had no intention of ever seeing him again.

And what the hell were the *McCready papers*?

He dashed to the lobby and had to cool his heels for fifteen minutes, waiting. One couple checking in, two checking out. At last, it was his turn.

He practically snatched the manila envelope from the desk clerk and found a semiprivate corner behind a potted plant. When he got his first look at the contents, despair washed over him. These were the documents Trent Matthews had tried to get him to sign at the lawyer's office after the meeting with Cal McCready. The papers Vaughn had flat-out refused.

But Brie didn't know that.

Vaughn shot to his feet, fury replacing his despair. He was going to fix this. Now. Fortunately for him, Trent Matthews happened to pick that very moment to slip out the front door. Vaughn followed on his heels.

"Going somewhere?" he asked menacingly.

Matthews turned and gasped. Every ounce of color left his face. "Blackwood. I thought you were at the party."

"I'll bet you did. You gate-crashed, right?"

The idiot lawyer had the balls to bristle with indignation. "It's not a crime. I'll pay Sophie for the meal if that's a problem."

"And Brie?" Vaughn asked silkily. "What will you do about Brie?"

Matthews goggled. "I didn't do anything to your woman. You can ask her. I was super polite."

Vaughn kept approaching. Trent kept backing up. Now the circular fountain blocked his escape. The large expanse of driveway with concrete and brick pavers was oddly empty save for two bored valets a couple hundred yards away who were smoking and trying to stay out of the sun.

"What did you say to her?" He took Matthews by the shirt collar and lifted him two inches.

Even then, the clueless lawyer tried to brazen his way through. "I told her you wanted her to sign the papers. She asked if you had seen them. I said yes. I did you a favor, man. You need to keep your eye on the prize. Broads and babies? They're nothing beside the money you can make on this deal."

"Damn you to hell, Matthews. You're fired. But I

don't suppose that matters to you, because I'm pretty damn sure you're on McCready's payroll. Am I right?"

The guilty flicker in Matthews's furtive gaze gave Vaughn his answer and blinded him with rage. He gave the slick lawyer a quick blow to the chin, toppling him over the low wall into the bubbling water.

Matthews cursed and floundered.

Vaughn's chest heaved. "And because you're on McCready's payroll, I'm texting him right now to let him know that his lackey is no longer employed by me."

Trent clambered to his feet, dripping and pathetic. "No, no. Don't do that. We'll work something out."

Vaughn hit Send. "Too late. There's nothing to work out. You and I are through, Matthews. The deal is off. Some things in life are more important than money."

While Vaughn strode toward the valets and produced his claim ticket, his brain whirled. When the car was brought around, he seated himself behind the wheel and squealed out of the exit. He had to fix this. But how?

He knew where to find Brie. Or he was fairly certain he did. She would be home by now, and Danika would be napping.

The reading on his speedometer slowed him down. Literally. He pulled off in a public parking area and tried to formulate a plan. First he needed to take care of some urgent business. Twenty minutes wouldn't make the situation better or worse. Brie wasn't going anywhere.

After two brief phone calls and three longer conversations, he felt the constriction in his chest ease. Now, at least his close friends and associates knew not to trust McCready and Matthews. The slimy duo had messed up badly this time. They might still be able to operate, but word was out. No reputable businessman or woman would give them the time of day.

Vaughn shifted into gear and pulled back out onto the highway. Ten minutes later, Brie's little house was a welcome sight. Her car, thankfully, was in the driveway. He parked behind it, hemming her in. No reason to give her an escape route.

He couldn't remember the last time he had been this nervous. As a rule, *he* was the one who made *other* people nervous.

Did he know what he was going to say? If he had to guess, he was pretty damn sure this was his last chance with Brielle Gunderson. A flub-up at this juncture would ruin everything.

He wiped his damp palms on his pants legs, got out and locked the car. Then he strode up the sidewalk and rang the bell. The baby slept with a small fan in her room for white noise. She wouldn't hear.

When the door opened without ceremony, his heart cracked wide-open. Brie had been crying. Dear God. And all because of him. Because he had given her no reason to doubt that he would draw up those papers or ask her to sign them.

"May I come in?" he asked quietly.

Brie had nothing left. Emotionally. Physically. This day had taken whatever energy and joy she had and flushed it down the drain.

As soon as Nika had fallen asleep, Brie lost the battle to keep her emotions under control. She had sobbed uncontrollably, grieving the loss of a dream that was never real in the first place.

She had hoped her note to Vaughn would be an end to things. Apparently, he still had something else to say.

"You'll miss your flight," she pointed out, not opening the door any wider.

He was gray faced and haggard, his posture slumped. She had never seen him like this. "Please, Brie. Let me in."

She lifted her shoulders and let them fall in a shrug of resignation. "Fine. Suit yourself." She had peeled out of her beautiful dress as soon as she got home. Now she was wearing faded gray sweatpants and an old concert T-shirt. If she had deliberately tried, she couldn't look any worse.

Not that Vaughn noticed. Once she let him in and moved toward the living room, he prowled, pacing back and forth.

Brie waited him out. She had said everything she had to say. If he was looking for an apology, he was out of luck.

Finally, after wearing a rut in her carpet, he sat in the chair opposite her spot on the sofa, leaving the coffee table between them. It reminded her of the coffee table where Nika had played soon after Vaughn discovered he had a daughter.

Today there was no child to defuse the tension.

Vaughn rubbed his face with his hands. "First off, those papers weren't from me."

She blinked. "Your name was on them."

"Not on the signature lines," he said curtly. "Matthews showed the papers to me the morning after the gala in Dallas. I told him to destroy the contract, plain and simple. He and McCready were worried that I was being distracted by personal matters, so when I said no, they went behind my back. As it turns out, McCready had Matthews on his payroll, too, and was pulling the strings. Do you believe me?"

The fire in his eyes was more like the Vaughn she knew. "Yes," she said. "I believe you. As it turns out, I wasn't willing to accept Matthews at face value, but when I asked him outright if you had seen the papers and he said yes, he really didn't seem to be lying. I didn't know what else to think."

"I did see them—so the only lie he told you was that I *wanted* you to sign them. His blend of truth and fiction must have been convincing."

She swallowed. "Yes. It was."

"I am sorry that happened to you," Vaughn said. "Sorrier than you know."

"I was humiliated," she admitted, wincing at the memory.

"Well, if it's any consolation, Trent Matthews ended up in the fountain at the Bellamy. I hope his humiliation outlasts yours. The skunk deserved it."

"How did he end up in the fountain?"

Vaughn shifted his gaze away, looking as guilty as a kid caught stealing a candy bar. "I might have punched him. Just once," he said hastily. "It wasn't a brawl."

Even in the midst of Brie's bleak grief, the image made her smile. "Fair enough. I should thank you, I guess."

"We need to talk," he said soberly.

"You mentioned that before, but I'm not sure why. You and I both know where things stand."

"No," he said carefully. "Not anymore."

"I'm confused."

Vaughn stood and paced again. "In my father's will, he said that I was the child who turned out most like him. When I read those words, I was furious. Shocked. Hurt. I've been processing that information for weeks now, and as much as it pains me to admit it, the old man was right. I didn't see it—but now that I do, I know I don't want to be this way anymore. It's not easy to turn things around. Even now, I'm struggling to change. But I want to, Brie. I don't want to be my father. I won't."

His eyes glittered with emotion when he turned back to face her.

Seeing him so hurt and vulnerable destroyed her. Despite everything he had done to break her heart, she couldn't bear to witness him like this. She went to him and hugged him the way she would comfort a hurting friend.

"You're *not* your father," she said. "I could have told him that. And for the record, Miranda and Kace never thought you were, or they wouldn't have released your portion of the inheritance."

"Maybe. Or maybe Miranda was tired of dealing with it."

"You're a good person, Vaughn. Single-minded, perhaps, but that quality has served you well in the business world."

He stepped back, breaking the embrace. But he took

both her hands in his. "I'd like another chance with you."

Her heart sank. "To what end? Everything will wind up exactly the same. We're too different."

"I've made some changes," he said slowly.

"I know. And it's been wonderful watching you with Nika. She brings out your softer side. I've enjoyed seeing your gentler, nurturing qualities."

"But?"

She pulled away, putting the distance of the room between them. "We've been over this a dozen times. I can't have a long-term affair with you. I have a daughter who has to be my first priority."

"And what if you and I were married?"

A sob lodged in her throat, making it hard to speak. "It wouldn't matter. A piece of paper won't solve our problems." The prospect he had raised was so unbelievably sweet that she wanted to throw caution to the wind. But it was dangerous.

His voice was low and determined when he spoke again, as if to underline the importance of what he was saying. "I resigned as vice president of the Dallas TCC this afternoon. I've called several of my key business associates and told them I'll be leaving the Fort Worth area, possibly selling off a big portion of my company."

"I don't understand."

He gave her a sweet, uncomplicated smile. "I'm moving back to Royal, Brie. To be near my daughter and the woman I love."

Her jaw dropped. "You love me?"

"Dear lord, sweetheart, you shouldn't even have to

ask. I can't believe I messed up so badly that you don't believe me when I finally say it. I'm the slowest man on the planet, but I can be taught, I swear. *Yes.* I love you. I'm fairly certain I always have. That's why it hurt so much when you ended our relationship and moved away. I told myself I didn't care. I kept on doing the things I knew how to do. But underneath it all, I was turning more into my father every day. Cold. Distant. Alone. I'm so sorry I let you down three years ago."

"Oh, Vaughn." She put her hands to her cheeks, caught up in a maelstrom of emotions. "You can't move to Royal. Your life is in Dallas and Fort Worth."

"It was," he conceded. "Now it's not. For one thing, apparently I own a bank."

"Small potatoes for a man like you."

He grinned. "Maybe I'll turn it into a financial empire. Once I sell off a chunk of Blackwood Energy, I'll have plenty of capital to invest. It will be a challenge."

"I see."

"Don't you want to ask me why I'm really moving back?" he said gently, closing the distance between them.

"I'm afraid to," she admitted.

He pulled her into his arms and rested his chin on top of her head with a long, weary sigh. "Don't be afraid, my sweet love. Not now. When the time is right, I'd like to marry you. And claim Danika legally. I want us to be a family. We'll build a big-ass house or maybe buy *another* ranch and give Kellan a run for his money. Whatever you want. In the meantime, I plan to make life a little easier for a full-time vet and a single mom."

She searched his face. "If this is a dream, don't wake me up."

He pinched her butt. Hard.

"Ow," Brie said.

"Are you convinced this is real?" His lopsided smile was the most beautiful thing she had ever seen.

"Kiss me, Vaughn. Make me believe it."

His lips were warm and firm, his body hard and perfect against hers. They were incredibly different as human beings, but where it counted, their hearts were perfectly in sync.

The kiss lingered, deepened.

Vaughn shuddered. "How much longer until Nika wakes up?"

Brie chuckled ruefully. "Not long enough."

"Damn." His long-faced expression amused her.

"But we have tonight," she reminded him. "If you can wait that long."

"Tonight and every night," he said, the words sounding like a vow. "Whatever life throws at us, Brielle Gunderson, we're a team now. I plan to love you until we're both old and wrinkled and cranky."

"Cranky?" She lifted an eyebrow.

"That will probably be me. But you'll always know how to tame your grumpy spouse, my love."

She looked him straight in the eyes, trying to communicate what was in her heart. "I don't want to tame you, Vaughn. I fell in love with the hard-edged guy who destroys me in the bedroom. You are who you are, and I adore you."

He kissed her again, hard and sweet and passionate all at the same time. “We’ll compromise, then,” he promised. “I’ll be fully domesticated as a husband and father and upstanding member of the community.”

“But when the lights go out?” she teased.

“All bets are off, Brie. All bets are off…”

* * * * *

COMING NEXT MONTH FROM

Available May 5, 2020

#2731 CLAIMED BY A STEELE

Forged of Steele • by Brenda Jackson

When it comes to settling down, playboy CEO Gannon Steele has a ten-year plan. And it doesn't include journalist Delphine Ryland. So why is he inviting her on a cross-country trip? Especially since their red-hot attraction threatens to do away with all his good intentions...

#2732 HER TEXAS RENEGADE

Texas Cattleman's Club: Inheritance • by Joanne Rock

When wealthy widow and business owner Miranda Dupree needs a security expert, there's only one person for the job—her ex, bad boy hacker Kai Maddox. It's all business until passions reignite, but will her old flame burn her a second time?

#2733 RUTHLESS PRIDE

Dynasties: Seven Sins • by Naima Simone

Putting family first, CEO Joshua Lowell abandoned his dreams to save his father's empire. When journalist Sophie Armstrong uncovers a shocking secret, he'll do everything in his power to shield his family from another scandal. But wanting her is a complication he didn't foresee...

#2734 SCANDALOUS REUNION

Lockwood Lightning • by Jules Bennett

Financially blackmailed attorney Maty Taylor must persuade her ex, Sam Hawkins, to sell his beloved distillery to his enemy. His refusal does nothing to quiet the passion between Maty and Sam. When powerful secrets are revealed, can their second chance survive?

#2735 AFTER HOURS SEDUCTION

The Men of Stone River • by Janice Maynard

When billionaire CEO Quinten Stone is injured, he reluctantly accepts live-in help at his remote home from assistant Katie Duncan—who he had a passionate affair with years earlier. Soon he's fighting his desire for the off-limits beauty as secrets from their past resurface...

#2736 SECRETS OF A FAKE FIANCÉE

The Stewart Heirs • by Yahrah St. John

Rejected by the family she wants to know, Morgan Stewart accepts Jared Robinson's proposal to pose as his fiancée to appease his own family. But when their fake engagement uncovers real passion, can Morgan have what she's always wanted, or will a vicious rumor derail everything?

SPECIAL EXCERPT FROM

HARLEQUIN

DESIRE

Putting family first, CEO Joshua Lowell abandoned his dreams to save his father's empire. When journalist Sophie Armstrong uncovers a shocking secret, he'll do everything in his power to shield his family and his pride from another scandal. But wanting her is a complication he didn't foresee...

Read on for a sneak peek at
Ruthless Pride
by USA TODAY *bestselling author Naima Simone*

"Stalking me, Ms. Armstrong?" he drawled, his fingers gripping his water bottle so tight, the plastic squeaked in protest.

He immediately loosened his hold. Damn, he'd learned long ago to never betray any weakness of emotion. People were like sharks scenting bloody chum in the water when they sensed a chink in his armor. But when in this woman's presence, his emotions seemed to leak through like a sieve. The impenetrable shield barricading him that had been forged in the fires of pain, loss and humiliation came away dented and scratched after an encounter with Sophie. And that presented as much of a threat, a danger to him, as her insatiable need to prove that he was a deadbeat father and puppet to a master thief.

"Stalking you?" she scoffed, bending down to swipe her own bottle of water and a towel off the ground. "Need I remind you, it was you who showed up at my job yesterday, not the other way around. So I guess that makes us even in the showing-up-where-we're-not-wanted department."

"Oh, we're not even close to anything that resembles even, Sophie," he said, using her name for the first time aloud. And damn if it didn't taste good on his tongue. If he didn't sound as if he were stroking the two syllables like they were bare, damp flesh.

"I hate to disappoint you and your dreams of narcissistic grandeur, but I've been a member of this gym for years." She swiped her towel over her throat and upper chest. "I've seen you here, but it's not my fault if you've never noticed me."

"That's bull," he snapped. "I would've noticed you."

The words echoed between them, the meaning in them pulsing like a thick, heavy heartbeat in the sudden silence that cocooned them. Her silver eyes flared wide before they flashed with…what? Surprise? Irritation? Desire. A liquid slide of lust prowled through him like a hungry—so goddamn hungry—beast.

HDEXP0420

The air simmered around them. How could no one else see it shimmer in waves from the concrete floor like steam from a sidewalk after a summer storm?

She was the first to break the visual connection, and when she ducked her head to pat her arms down, the loss of her eyes reverberated in his chest like a physical snapping of tautly strung wire. He fisted his fingers at his side, refusing to rub the echo of soreness there.

"Do you want me to pull out my membership card to prove that I'm not some kind of stalker?" She tilted her head to the side. "I'm dedicated to my job, but I refuse to cross the line into creepy…or criminal."

He ground his teeth against the apology that shoved at his throat, but after a moment, he jerked his head down in an abrupt nod. "I'm sorry. I shouldn't have jumped to conclusions." And then because he couldn't resist, because it still gnawed at him when he shouldn't have cared what she—a reporter—thought of him or not, he added, "That predilection seems to be in the air."

She narrowed her eyes on him, and a tiny muscle ticked along her delicate but stubborn jaw. Why that sign of temper and forced control fascinated him, he opted not to dwell on. "And what is that supposed to mean?" she asked, the pleasant tone belied by the anger brewing in her eyes like gray storm clouds.

Moments earlier, he'd wondered if fury or desire had heated her gaze.

God help him, because masochistic fool that he'd suddenly become, he craved them both.

He wanted her rage, her passion…wanted both to beat at him, heat his skin, touch him. Make him feel.

Mentally, he scrambled away from that, that need, like it'd reared up and flashed its fangs at him. The other man he'd been—the man who'd lost himself in passion, paint and life captured on film—had drowned in emotion. Willingly. Joyfully. And when it'd been snatched away—when that passion, that life—had been stolen from him by cold, brutal reality, he'd nearly crumbled under the loss, the darkness. Hunger, wanting something so desperately, led only to the pain of eventually losing it.

He'd survived that loss once. Even though it'd been like sawing off his own limbs. He might be an emotional amputee, but dammit, he'd endured. He'd saved his family, their reputation and their business. But he'd managed it by never allowing himself to need again.

And Sophie Armstrong, with her pixie face and warrior spirit, wouldn't undo all that he'd fought and silently screamed to build.